A plan takes root.

Quickly, I began to read. "Says they can live for thousands of years and that there are nine species. And some ancient Arabian legend claims the reason it looks the way it does is because the devil plucked up the baobab, thrust its branches into the earth, and left its roots in the air."

Quincy joined in, "And it's the national tree of Madagascar."

"Has a lot of names . . . bottle tree, upside-down tree, monkey bread tree, and tree of life," I added.

"And it's one of the top seven endangered trees in the world," he read.

Abruptly, I stopped reading. "Endangered?" I repeated. When it came to plants and trees, being endangered made my daddy take notice. For a moment, I wondered if Daddy had ever even heard of baobab trees. There was nothing in his computer files.

Number One Way to Get More Attention
in the Reindeer House

1. Save a tree from possible extinction!

Quincy turned away from the computer screen toward me. We locked eyes. "You're way too quiet, Zoe. What're you thinking?"

Other Books You May Enjoy

Zoe
IN WONDERLAND

BRENDA WOODS

PUFFIN BOOKS

PUFFIN BOOKS
An imprint of Penguin Random House LLC
375 Hudson Street
New York, New York 10014

First published in the United States of America by Nancy Paulsen Books, 2016
Published by Puffin Books, an imprint of Penguin Random House LLC, 2017

THE LIBRARY OF CONGRESS HAS CATALOGED THE NANCY PAULSEN BOOKS EDITION AS FOLLOWS:
Names: Woods, Brenda (Brenda A.) author.
Title: Zoe in wonderland / Brenda Woods.
Description: New York, NY : Nancy Paulsen Books, [2016]
Summary: "Introverted, daydream-prone Zoe is afraid her real life will never be as
exciting as her imaginary one"—Provided by publisher. Identifiers: LCCN 2015044622 |
ISBN 9780399170973 (hardback)
Subjects: | CYAC: African Americans—Fiction. | Imagination—Fiction.
| Families—Fiction. | Self-confidence—Fiction. | BISAC: JUVENILE FICTION /
Family / General (see also headings under Social Issues). | JUVENILE FICTION /
Social Issues / Friendship. | JUVENILE FICTION /
People & Places / United States / African American.
Classification: LCC PZ7.W86335 Zo 2016 | DDC [Fic]—dc23
LC record available at https://lccn.loc.gov/2015044622

Puffin Books ISBN 9780425288917

Printed in the United States of America

1 3 5 7 9 10 8 6 4 2

Edited by Nancy Paulsen
Design by Annie Ericsson

For Dominic

1

Four Things That Definitely Aren't My Fault

The first thing that's definitely not my fault is that our last name is Reindeer. No one, not even Grandpa Reindeer, is quite sure how that came to be the family name. And even though everyone complains about it—well, everyone except my daddy—no one ever did anything to change it. As for me, I get tired of the jokes, especially around Christmastime.

Once, last year, I explained to Grandpa and Nana Reindeer how you can actually go to court and legally change your name, but they both stared at me like I'd just said a cussword. Then Nana Reindeer shook her finger at me the way she used to when I was little and I'd done something bad and whispered, "Hush, Zoe, with that modern nonsense. Like it or not, it's our name."

The second thing that's definitely not my fault is that my daddy, Mr. Darrow Reindeer, is a horticulturist, which is a fancy way to say he knows a bunch of stuff about growing flowers and plants and trees. And because I'm the only one of his three kids who's interested in learning about it, he's teaching it to me.

The third thing that's not my fault either is that we live in a house behind my daddy's business in Pasadena, California, which is called:

Doc Reindeer's Exotic Plant Wonderland

And if anyone ever asks why he named it that, he informs them that he's a doctor of plants and this is his wonderland.

The last thing I cannot and will never be able to take responsibility for is the fact that I have an extremely annoying older sister, Jade, and an even more annoying younger brother, Harper. That puts me, Zoe G. Reindeer, smack-dab in the middle. The G. stands for Gabrielle. It's also my mom's name.

I have to admit there are two things that are my fault.

Two Things That Absolutely Are My Fault

1. I did send away for the seeds.
2. I didn't read the directions before I planted them.

And not reading the directions led to *the sign* that changed everything.

Now—about the seeds . . .

2

Sort of Like a Seed

The outside of a seed has a hard coat or shell, and the inside, which Daddy says is called an embryo, comes alive when you water it. Sort of like a seed, there's this thing inside of me that's nothing like my outside, and it's alive.

Some days it comes alive a lot, and other days it happens maybe only once or twice, kind of like a sneeze or hiccup.

Sometimes it keeps me from paying attention. And not paying attention can get me into humongous trouble— trouble that wraps around me tighter than a cocoon and is almost impossible to wriggle out of.

I really never know when it's going to come alive, but once it gets going, it's kind of like a bowling ball that's rolling faster than fast down the lane toward the pins—impossible to stop.

Like yesterday, for example.

After school, I was walking home past the park where a girls' soccer game was being played. I was on a soccer team once, but I quickly found out that I stink at sports. So I did what most people do who stink at sports: I quit. But sometimes it's fun to watch, so I stopped and stared through the chain-link fence. The players' feet were tangled around the ball, everyone trying to get control.

And suddenly, it—the thing that's inside of me, which I guess you could call my wild imagination—came alive and she—*Imaginary Zoe*—appeared.

Zoe G. Reindeer, super forward, was on the field with the ball, in a perfect position. Her eyes zeroed in on the goal. She aimed and kicked with all of her might. The ball zoomed through the air. Their tall goalkeeper stretched sideways like she was made of rubber, trying desperately to guard the net, but she failed, and the ball crossed the goal line. Zoe's teammates hoisted her in the air!

When the buzzer signaling the end of the game sounded, I blinked, and just like that, the real Zoe was back. The real me was still peering at the players through the fence, watching the winning team give each other high fives. The real me still stunk at sports and was now going to be late getting home from school.

The real me, a shy, perfectly plain girl-person, wears glasses. The real me never stands out, not at school, not at home, not at anywhere. The real me doesn't like loud crowds. Mostly, the real me likes the quiet of the Wonderland's pond and greenhouse and of half-empty movie theaters. The real me has only one friend. Plus the real me has big feet, feet that make me resemble the letter *L*. The real me can't even whistle. If they gave awards for being boring, I'd get a gold medal.

But *Imaginary Zoe* is everything the real me isn't. Instead of being eleven years old, she's already a teenager and even has her driver's license. She's really pretty and can sing and dance and has friends who hover around her like a flock of pigeons, and she gets really good grades without studying a lot, and she never forgets things, and everyone loves her, especially her parents and brother and sister and even teachers. Plus she doesn't stink at sports.

Sometimes I try very hard to keep *Imaginary Zoe* from disappearing, but because my real world keeps interrupting with all of its stuff like chores and homework and getting annoyed and having to brush my teeth and sometimes being forced to eat pickled beets, *Imaginary Zoe* vanishes.

෴

Now that I've explained how I'm sort of like a seed and also about *Imaginary Zoe*, I can tell you about the real seeds.

3

A Very Tall Man

It was a Saturday and the rain was starting and stopping, coming and going, like someone was up there in the clouds playing with a switch, turning it off and on, on and off. The sun was playing hide-and-seek too, every now and then shining a little light through the clouds before quickly disappearing again.

My mom had just left to pick up my sister, Jade-queen-bee-of-the-house, from cheerleading practice and to drop off my brother, Harper-science-geek-genius, at his museum class. I was inside the nursery, doing my regular Saturday jobs: watering the plants, pruning away dead leaves, spraying the orchids with purified water. After that, I usually organize the bulbs and make certain all of the seed packets are in their right places and lined right side up. Then I head to the greenhouse, my favorite quiet place, especially when it rains.

Grandpa Reindeer was there because Daddy was heading out to the desert and he needed someone to be at the register.

"I know how to work the register," I'd told my daddy. "Can I, please, please, please?"

But he'd responded the way he always does. "No, Zoe, you're only eleven."

Only eleven. I was getting tired of being only eleven. "When I'm twelve, can I do it?" I asked.

"Maybe."

Daddy climbed into his beat-up white truck. "Thanks for helping me out, Pops," he told Grandpa.

He was going to buy two rare endangered plants, one called a baseball plant and the other one called an old woman cactus. For the past week, it's all he's talked about. The way some people are concerned about endangered animals, my daddy is concerned about endangered plants.

"I should be back by five. I doubt we'll have many customers in this weather. And keep an eye on Zoe."

Grandpa glanced my way and winked.

Keep an eye on me? I really don't need anyone to keep an eye on me, I thought. Besides, only chameleons and other weird things can keep one eye on anything. Humans are on the two-eye system. Where one eye goes, the other follows.

I waved at Daddy, but I suppose he didn't see me. His truck wheels rolled over puddles, making tracks in the muddy gravel, and he was gone.

Not long after Grandpa sat down, he nodded off, the way he has a habit of doing. I was at the sink, filling the watering can, staring at the register, when suddenly—

Zoe was the Saturday boss of the Wonderland. She liked being in charge. She popped open the register and counted the money. She wrote down the total. Then she jotted down ideas for increasing sales. She'd show the list to her daddy when he got back and he'd give her a raise. She certainly deserved one. How much? Zoe wondered.

When the bell that chimes whenever someone opens the nursery door went *ding-dong*, I blinked. The watering can I was holding was overflowing with water. Quickly, I turned off the faucet.

The man standing in the doorway was so tall, he had to duck to get inside. My eyes started at his red-and-white two-toned shoes, and by the time they reached his smiling lips, my head was cranked all the way back, resting on my shoulders. He was that tall.

His skin was dark brown and his teeth gleamed like they'd been painted glossy white. His raincoat was gray, his pants pale yellow, and his black cap had the letters JPL on it.

Grandpa woke up, yawned, and stumbled to his feet. "Can I help you?" he asked the man.

The man turned his head slowly, scanning the room. "I was passing by and wondered if you have a tree I've been looking for but haven't been able to find. It's something quite unusual for these parts."

The man spoke with an accent I didn't recognize. It wasn't Spanish, maybe French—but if you want to know the truth, except for movies, I haven't heard many French people talk.

Grandpa turned on the computer at the end of the counter. "If you tell me the name, I can check our inventory and see if we have it. We have a boat-load of unusual things here. That's why it's called a Wonderland."

"I'm searching for a baobab tree," he said.

"Baobab tree?" Grandpa repeated.

"*B-A-O-B-A-B*," the tall man spelled it out.

Grandpa Reindeer typed in the letters, but nothing came up. "I don't think we have any." He typed it

11

in again. "Nope . . . nothing, sorry. What kind of tree is it?"

"It's a tree that grows in my country, Madagascar."

I glanced up at his face. His lips were almost as dark as his skin. I'm usually too shy to talk to strangers, but I had to ask, so I said, "You're all the way from . . ." Suddenly my shyness got stronger than my curiosity and my words stopped.

Grandpa looked my way and reminded me, the way he and Nana have since I was little, "Don't be bashful, Zoe."

I started over. "You're all the way from Madagascar?"

"Yes," the man replied.

"Wow. I've imagined myself there before," I told him.

"Imagined yourself?" he asked.

I nodded and glanced at Grandpa. His smile encouraged me to keep talking. "When I was a little kid, I saw that movie called *Madagascar* probably four times, plus last year for geography our teacher showed us a video, so it was pretty easy to imagine myself there."

The tall man raised one eyebrow and grinned at me.

"It looked like a beautiful place, plus it has some animals and plants that can't be found anywhere else on Earth. That's what the video said," I informed him.

"It is beautiful," the man agreed.

"B-A-O-B-A-B." Grandpa wrote it on a slip of paper. "Well, I've never heard of it, but I'm sure my son has. He's got what I call a wealth of knowledge."

The tall man said, "It's also called 'the tree of life.' They can live for thousands of years. Or maybe it's listed under another name? Try 'monkey bread tree.'"

I laughed.

Grandpa typed in *monkey bread tree*. "Sorry, no monkey bread tree, but there is something called a monkey cup plant. It says it's an insect eater."

"I'll try somewhere else," the man replied, then turned to leave.

"Sorry to say this, Mister, but if it's unique and it grows and you can't find it here, you're probably not going to find it anywhere close by. I'm not trying to brag, but we've got some very weird stuff, even Venus flytraps and cobra lilies and . . ."

The very tall man laughed loudly, opening his mouth so wide, I could see his pink tonsils. "Thank you for your time, sir."

Grandpa eyed the cap and asked him, "You work over at JPL?"

"Yes. For almost twenty years."

"What's JPL?" I asked.

Grandpa answered, "Jet Propulsion Lab up the road, other side of Altadena. Place that sends probes and

13

instruments out into space, studies planets . . . among other things."

"That's right," the tall man agreed. "I'm an astronomer."

My curiosity wouldn't give up. "An astronomer? So you know a lot of stuff about outer space?" I asked.

He looked my way, pointed up to the sky, and answered, "Yes, we imagine ourselves up there. Having a community open house next month, if anyone might be interested." His eyes stared into mine. "The information is all online . . . young people sure seem to enjoy it."

The astronomer smiled again, and as he opened the door to leave, the chime sounded and the sun suddenly burst out of its hiding place. "The star of day finally returns," he said.

The star of day? I'd never heard the sun called that before.

"I'll leave a message for my son about the baobab. Is there some way he can get in touch with you?" Grandpa asked.

"I'll stop by again. It's on my way," the tall man answered.

I went to the door, but with legs as long as his, legs like stilts, he'd already made it to his car and was climbing inside. There was a peace sign decal on the back window, and when he started his car, the tailpipe sputtered and smoked.

"Rather odd fellow," Grandpa commented.

I squinted at the sun—the star of day. "I like him," I said.

And just as the tall man zoomed off, Mom drove up.

4

Just Zoe

My sister, Jade, was in the passenger seat, and a girl I'd never seen before was sitting in the back—probably a new princess friend of Jade's or maybe another queen bee. I keep wondering how Jade does it, collecting friends the way I used to collect Barbie dolls. Nana Reindeer calls it "Jade's gift."

Jade is fifteen, tall and kind of skinny except for her butt, which is sort of big, but she's always doing exercises trying to make it bigger. She has brown hair and huge dark eyes. Even without mascara, her lashes are so long that I sometimes wonder how she keeps her eyes open. Any girl who wants to avoid attention should try having Jade Reindeer for a sister. With Jade in a room, most other girls disappear, especially me.

Jade's friend climbed out of the car, her eyes darting around the Wonderland. Jade looked embarrassed, because unlike me, she hates living here and is constantly begging to move somewhere normal.

Jade frowned. "Welcome to the Weirdland," she muttered.

"It's not called the Weirdland . . . It's called the Wonderland," I told her.

Jade sneered at me. "Whatever . . . plant girl."

Jade thinks it hurts my feelings when she calls me that, but it doesn't. I love taking care of the plants and watching them grow. As far as I'm concerned, I could live in the Wonderland forever and ever and ever.

The new-Jade-friend looked me over and asked, "Who are you?"

Jade gave me a snide sideways glance and answered, "Her? . . . Oh, that's *just Zoe.*"

Just Zoe?

"Your little sister?" the girl inquired.

"Yeah, *just Zoe.*"

Pink gloss on the girl's lips glistened. She smiled and said, "Hey, Zoe, I'm Torrey."

Unlike Jade's usual friends, who mostly treat me

like I'm invisible, she seemed nice. "Hey, Torrey," I replied.

Mom interrupted. "Zoe, help me with these groceries."

I frowned. "Me? What about Jade?"

Jade smirked and headed toward the house. "Have to study."

"I can help you, Mrs. Reindeer," Torrey offered. Right then, I knew Torrey was a princess and not a queen bee. Sometimes it can be hard to tell the difference, but one thing you can be certain of is this: queen bees never volunteer to help.

"That's okay, Torrey. There's not that much. You two go study."

I laughed. "Yeah, right, Mom. News alert—Jade never studies."

"Stop it, Zoe," Mom whispered.

"But I still have work to do in the nursery," I whined.

Mom gave me the stop-whining-and-do-what-I-say look.

And so, I helped bring the groceries in the house.

I'd just grabbed the last bag and was lifting it to the kitchen counter when the paper handle broke.

Mom said, "Tell me that's not the bag with the eggs."

I checked the contents of the bag and spotted the eggs. "Wrong," I informed her.

"Then at least tell me they're not broken, Zoe."

I opened the carton of eggs. Most were broken. "Wrong again."

"Zoe!" Mom snapped, "You have to be more careful!"

"You can't blame me for the handles ripping. It's not my fault. The bags are cheap."

Mom took a deep breath. "Next time, hold the bag from the bottom, Zoe."

"It's not my fault," I repeated.

After I helped put away the groceries and disposed of the broken eggs, I made a beeline to the bathroom. I was heading back to the nursery to finish up my work when I stopped and stared at myself in the hallway's full-length mirror. All of a sudden—

Zoe was wearing a purple vest with silver buttons, a hot-pink miniskirt, black leggings, and ankle boots. Her flat-ironed hair was flawless, and crystal earrings dangled from her ears. Her full lips, painted bright red, had the perfect pout . . .

But Jade appeared from her room, interrupting my fantasy. Torrey was right behind her. Of course,

Jade ignored me, but at least Torrey smiled as they headed for the kitchen. They must have been putting on makeup, because Jade looked even more gorgeous than usual.

The real me stared back from the mirror and wondered if parents only have a certain amount of stuff to pass on to their kids when they're helping to create them. Stuff like beauty. I supposed that because Jade was first, they'd given most of it to her, not knowing I might show up later and need some beauty too. It isn't fair. Jade is exactly right. I'm *just Zoe.*

On the way back to the nursery, I tripped on one of the uneven bricks along the pathway and almost fell. I glared down at my big feet. "Please stop growing!" I pleaded.

"Zoe?" Mom said, startling me. She was standing not far from me, about to get in the car.

"Huh?"

"Are you talking to yourself?" she asked.

"No."

She narrowed her eyes and stared at me, the way she does when she thinks one of us is lying.

"I wasn't. I swear."

"Okay . . . I'm going to the museum. Harper is presenting his science project. Do you want to come?" Mom asked as she climbed into the car.

And sit there listening to boy genius rattle on about his gadgets? I don't think so. "No, I promised Daddy," I told her. "Plus I have to take care of the stuff in the greenhouse, and I'm going to the movies with Quincy, remember?"

Mom glanced at her watch, said, "Right. See you later," and was off again. The gravel was still wet and her wheels made a gritty sound as they turned into the street.

And for the time being, I forgot about the tall man and the baobab trees and the star of day.

5

Quincy

After I finished in the nursery, I headed over to the greenhouse. The rain seemed like it had stopped for good because the sky was filling up with blue and the sun was still out. It was beginning to get warm, the way it sometimes is in Pasadena in October. Already, the water on the walkways was evaporating and the bees were back at work, buzzing around flowers. A sprinkling of people wandered in and around. Birds chirped songs, and colorful butterflies fluttered, and I felt happy to live at the Wonderland with its trees every shade of green, a pond with a stone mermaid fountain resting inside, and rock-lined winding paths. Like me with my daydreams, it's different. I know it's called Doc Reindeer's Exotic Plant Wonderland, but in my mind, I think of it as Zoe's Wonderland too, with its flowers that smell like perfume—especially gardenias and honeysuckle. And except for the birds' songs, it's very quiet in the morning, but once darkness comes, its night sounds take over.

Five Things I Love About the Wonderland

1. Studying a green velvety caterpillar inching slowly across a tree branch or having ladybugs land on me, which is sure to bring good luck—at least that's what Nana claims.
2. Staring at the lotus plants and lilies in the garden pond while the water ripples.
3. Watching cowardly lizards as they flee under rocks or logs as soon as a foot lands close by.
4. Spying a hawk landing at the pond's edge, taking a few sips, then flapping away. Me gazing upward as it spreads its wings and soars.
5. And at night, with beams of moonlight shining, hearing what sounds like more than a hundred crickets.

Five Things That Gross Me Out in the Wonderland

1. All spiders (except daddy longlegs).
2. Big beetles.
3. Red ants.
4. Anything that stings or bites.
5. Feeding the Venus flytraps, pitcher plants, and other carnivorous stuff.

As I stepped inside the greenhouse, I inhaled the smell of its flowers and wet soil and moss. The screen door shut behind me. As usual, it was cool inside, and the glass was still wet from the rain.

I was staring up through the greenhouse's glass roof when the door creaked open. It was Quincy—my one and only very best friend.

Quincy Hill and I have been best friends since kindergarten. He lives two blocks up the street, but unlike me, he doesn't have a brother or sister, and last year his parents got a divorce and his dad moved away to San Francisco. We've always gone to the same school and we're in the same grade, and this year, the first year of middle school, we're mostly in the same classes. We're exactly the same height and we both wear nerd glasses. His thick black frames take up most of his face. He's the only person I never, ever feel shy around.

"Hey, Prancer," he said, and grinned.

Because I know he's not trying to be mean, he's the only person I never get mad at for making reindeer jokes. All day yesterday, he called me Cupid.

"Hey, Quincy."

"You almost done?" he asked.

"Not even. I just got started."

"That's okay. The movie doesn't start till two." He glanced at his watch. "We have lots of time." His camera, as usual, was dangling from his neck.

Saturday movies with Quincy are one of my most favorite things. They're better than red velvet cupcakes with cream cheese icing, rocky road ice cream—better than anything my wild imagination cooks up. When Quincy grows up, he plans to go to film school and become a director. He says he'll hire me as a producer. Lately, at the end of movies, during the credits, I've started to picture my name there.

He hurried over to the terrarium that has the carnivorous plants. "Do you need me to feed them some grasshoppers or beetles?" Unlike me, Quincy enjoys that chore. But today, he was out of luck.

"My daddy already fed them this morning."

"I'm going to take some pictures of them, okay?" he asked.

"Like I would say no. You're my best friend, Quincy,"

I replied. Right then, I stopped what I was doing. "Hey, am I *just Zoe*?" I asked him.

"Huh?"

"You know . . . nothing special . . . almost a no-body . . . a zero."

"You, a zero? No way. You are Zoe G. Reindeer, future spectacular movie producer."

That made me smile. "Yeah, or maybe I'll be the Queen of the Wonderland, or both."

He snapped a few more pictures and started yapping. "Did you know reindeer's eyes change colors with the seasons? They change from golden green in the summer to blue in the winter. And they're the only mammals that can see ultraviolet light. I read that online."

"Yay!" I clapped my hands. "More interesting facts about reindeer that don't matter to most people, including me." Quincy, who calls himself a master of trivia, knows entirely too much about all kinds of things, including reindeer. "You know I hate my name!"

"Once you're eighteen, you can always change it, Zoe."

"I know this."

"But if I were you, I wouldn't. Wish my last name was Reindeer—that way, when I become a director, no one would ever forget my name. Quincy Reindeer. The name by itself would make me famous."

"You can have it. We'll trade names. I'll take your last name. Zoe Hill. It sounds normal, huh?"

He scrunched up his face. "Ahh . . . who wants a normal name?"

"Me," I replied.

6

Saving Tears

As soon as I finished up in the greenhouse, I made a beeline to the house to grab my backpack and jacket.

"Where're you goin' in such a hurry?" Jade asked. She and Torrey were in the kitchen, digging into a platter of nachos. Music blared and their bodies were moving with it.

"To the movies with Quincy," I answered.

Jade snickered. "A little date?"

Like a mad dog, I snarled at my sister, then grabbed a tortilla chip from the platter. "Not a date . . . nowhere near a date . . . He's my best friend," I claimed.

"Keep your dirty hands out of my food!" Jade ordered.

I examined my nails. While I was working in the

greenhouse, I'd forgotten to wear my gloves, as usual, so they were crusted black with dirt.

"It won't hurt you," I informed Jade as I washed my hands. "It's organic," I added, heading for the door.

Jade turned up her nose at me. "Thanks for the info, plant girl. Have fun on your little date."

I glared at my sister. "Not a date!"

Jade and Torrey shared that look—that you're-a-goofy-little-kid-and-we're-not look.

Then, Jade gave me her absolute best queen-bee smirk. And that was when—

Zoe became a diabolical magician. She held a remote-control device with special powers—the power to silence irritating pests. Zoe aimed it at Jade and pressed the button. "You're forever on mute," Zoe informed her. Jade struggled to speak but couldn't. Zoe cackled uncontrollably. "I can't hear you, sister dear!"

"Earth calling Zoe," Jade said, snapping me back to reality.

"Huh?"

"BG, Zoe . . . be gone," Jade said, and waved the back of her hand like she was shooing me away from her kingdom.

Jade has a lot of talents, and one of them is her ability to hurt my feelings without really trying, which gets me extremely mad and makes me feel as helpless as a prisoner with her hands and feet tied. I used to get so hurt that I'd cry. But that was like adding a log to the fire, giving her fuel. And the last thing a queen bee needs is more power.

A while back, Nana warned me that I was wasting my tears on silliness when I cried too much. Tears, she claims, should be saved for stuff that really matters. So I made a vow that Jade would never make me cry again, and instead I give her my mad-dog look. It doesn't shut her up, but it saves me lots of tears—tears I figure I'll need for the really sad things that could happen later.

I glanced over my shoulder, gave her my maddest dog look, grabbed my backpack, and did as I'd been commanded, but slammed the screen door as hard as I could.

Inside, Jade howled with laughter.

More than anything, I really hate it when people laugh at me.

Be quiet! I wanted to scream, but I didn't, because just then a thought came softly into my mind like a feather floating.

Be quiet = BQ.

7

Zoe Remembers

*D*oing the same thing over and over, Saturday after Saturday, seems like it would get boring, but with Quincy, it never does.

We climbed aboard the bus and headed to Old Pasadena.

Quincy is mostly in charge of movie picks because he reads reviews.

"What's it about?" I asked as we stood in the ticket line.

"Two people who meet on an airplane and discover they have something in common . . . a secret."

"Not a love story, I hope . . . I hate love stories."

"Definitely not a love story."

"Good."

We bought popcorn and sodas and had just snuggled into our seats when the lights dimmed and the previews began.

But when the movie started, I frowned. "You promised."

"What?" he answered innocently.

"No more movies with subtitles. If I wanted to read, I'd pick up a book."

"It's highly recommended, Zoe. Give it a chance."

"Okay . . . but next time a normal movie. Promise?"

He faked a yawn. "Normal . . . boring."

I pinched his arm.

"Ouch!"

"Promise me, Quincy."

"Shhhh," said the lady beside us.

So, we shut up, watched the French film, read the English words, ate the buttered popcorn, and sipped soda.

∽

"Now tell me you didn't like it," he said as we walked down Colorado Boulevard, stopping now and then to look around in the shops. "The plot twists were amazing. And I know you didn't expect that ending."

Sometimes I hate it when he's right, but this time he was. "The ending was pretty cool."

Quincy grinned and raised his fist to the sky, as if he'd won a victory. "See? Does Quincy Hill know movies or what?"

"You really are a dork. Really are!"

On the bus ride home, we decided to do what the actors had done in a scene from the movie: they'd picked out a person at random and tried to guess what kind of work they did or, if they were old, what kind of work they used to do. I went first.

I nudged Quincy, then pointed to an old man wearing a plaid hat and two-tone brown leather shoes. Because he was carrying a book, I whispered, "I bet he works in a bookstore."

We both stretched our necks to see the title of the book he was carrying. It said *A Mechanic's Guide to Classic Cars.*

"Hmmm." Quincy looked the man over from head to foot and disagreed. "Maybe a mechanic."

But before we could ask the man with the two-toned shoes if we were right, the bus slowed to a stop and the man stood up to get off. I fixed my eyes on his shoes and suddenly thought about the man who'd come looking for baobab trees.

"Oh! I almost forgot," I blurted.

"Forgot what?"

"About the really tall man who came to the nursery this morning. He's an astronomer from Madagascar."

"Huh?"

I gazed out the window at the sun. "He called the sun 'the star of day.'"

Quincy's eyes bounced from me to the sun and back to me again. "The star of day? Awesome!"

"He was looking for something called a baobab tree, but we didn't have any."

He shrugged. "Baobab tree? Never heard of it. I'll have to look it up."

"He said they grow in Madagascar," I told him. "Remember—that place in the movie?"

"Wonder what they look like?" we said at exactly the same time, then laughed.

As we stepped off the bus, I began taking long strides, trying to get home fast. I began to get ahead of him.

"What's the hurry, Zoe? Jeez!"

I slowed down and Quincy began blabbering. "Did you know a reindeer can't pee and walk at the same time?"

My elbow nudged him, knocking him slightly off balance. I wasn't mad, but I wanted to focus on other things. Things like baobab trees. "Not now, Quincy."

He grinned. "Okay, Blitzen."

8

Introducing the Snox

$\mathcal{T}$hankfully, when we got back to my house, Jade and Torrey were gone. I really didn't want Quincy to hear any of her date jokes.

With Quincy sitting beside me, I looked up *baobab tree* on the computer. Unexpectedly, there were a bunch of sites. I popped on one that called it "the tree of life" and a photo came up of about thirty baobab trees growing in a grassy Madagascar plain. The clear blue sky behind the trees made them look strangely beautiful. "Wow!"

"Yeah, wow!" he echoed.

I studied the tall, fat trunks and leafy branches closely.

Quincy said exactly what I was thinking: "Kinda different but very awesome."

We left that site and went to another. Quickly, I began to read. "Says they can live for thousands of years and that there are nine species. And some ancient Arabian legend claims the reason it looks the way it does is because the devil plucked up the baobab, thrust its branches into the earth, and left its roots in the air."

Quincy joined in, "And it's the national tree of Madagascar."

"Has a lot of names . . . bottle tree, upside-down tree, monkey bread tree, and tree of life," I added.

"And it's one of the top seven endangered trees in the world," he read.

Abruptly, I stopped reading. "Endangered?" I repeated. When it came to plants and trees, being endangered made my daddy take notice. For a moment, I wondered if Daddy had ever even heard of baobab trees. There was nothing in his computer files.

Number One Way to Get More Attention
in the Reindeer House

1. Save a tree from possible extinction!

Quincy turned away from the computer screen toward me. We locked eyes. "You're way too quiet, Zoe. What're you thinking?"

Because the wheels in my mind were turning fast, as fast as the wheels of a speeding bicycle, I ignored him.

"Tell me what you're thinking!" he demanded.

I inspected the picture of the tree of life again, beamed, and replied, "How to save the baobab trees from extinction, of course."

He chuckled. "Of course."

And that was when the front door opened and Harper, also known as *the snox*, strode in.

Harper is small for a nine-year-old, with dark brown hair and a pointy nose. He likes to wear hats and has quite a collection. Today he had on a gray derby.

Three Things You Need to Know
About Harper Reindeer

1. When he was younger, we mostly got along, and I used to let him come in my room whenever he wanted to and I even read to him, but after everyone discovered that he was extremely smart and he got transferred to the school for smart kids, he started treating me like I was dumb or something. I know I'm nowhere near as smart as he is, but I'm not dumb.

2. Last year I told him about an idea I had for a science project, and the next thing I knew, he claimed it was his idea and that idea got him to the finals at the science fair.

3. Every now and then I used to find him snooping in my desk, rummaging around, looking for I don't know what, so I banished him from my room and we've hardly ever had any real conversations since.

"Hey, Quincy," Harper said.

As usual, he'd acknowledged Quincy but ignored me.

"Hey, Harper," he replied.

"What're you guys doing?" Harper asked, craning his neck like a nosy giraffe, trying hard to get a look at the computer screen.

Because I feared he'd find some way to steal my idea again, before his eyes could zero in, I quickly minimized the site. "Nothing important," I replied.

My brother gave me a look that said, *Don't even think about trying to fool me, Zoe.* For several seconds, Harper glared at me and I glared back. Neither of us blinked.

Harper glanced at the computer once more, then slithered down the hallway to his room.

"Why'd you lie?" Quincy asked me.

"Because he's a snox."

He wrinkled his forehead like he was searching for a memory. "Oh yeah, I remember when you called him that after he stole your science idea."

"Exactly. He's the sneakiest person I know, but he's also extremely smart . . . smart like a fox. *Sneaky* plus *fox* equals *snox*. He'd find some way to make this baobab tree idea his, and it isn't. It's mine. Understand?"

Quincy nodded in agreement. "Understand."

I might even get some attention, I was thinking when—

Zoe was standing at the podium. The auditorium was packed and reporters pointed video cameras at the guest of honor: environmentalist Zoe G. Reindeer. At the end of Zoe's inspiring speech, people clapped and began popping up around the room like popcorn until finally everyone was standing. Single-handedly, Zoe had saved the baobabs from certain extinction. The gold medal was placed around her neck. In the audience, her father cheered and her mother cried.

Quincy tapped my shoulder. "Zoe?"

"What?"

"You sorta zoned out. Are you all right?" he asked.

I nodded. "Just thinking."

"About what?" he asked.

Imaginary Zoe was difficult to explain, and I'd never talked about her to anyone, not even Quincy. She was my secret. "Stuff," I replied.

"You've been doing that a lot lately . . . like you stop listening."

Quincy was right. *Imaginary Zoe* had been showing up more and more, making me miss things like homework assignments and teachers' questions and Reindeer-parent orders.

"It's just my imagination," I tried to explain.

"Oh," he said, but I could tell by the look in his eyes that he didn't understand.

I tried again. "I imagine cool stuff."

"Like fantasizing?" He'd named it just right.

"Exactly," I told him.

"Awesome."

9

Daddy Reindeer

$\mathcal{T}$he snox was still in his room, but the strange thing about the snox is I never really know when he might appear from out of nowhere, snooping, peeking around corners, being a total pest. For that reason, I quickly went back to the baobab sites, printed several pages of pictures and articles about them, sneaked to my room, and stashed the pages under my mattress. That way, I'd have something to read privately later on.

Quincy and I were nestled side by side, searching for more and more facts about baobabs, when Mom stepped through the kitchen door. "Hi, Zoe . . . Hi, Quincy," she called out.

"Hey," we replied, neither of us glancing up, our eyes

remaining glued on the PC screen, scanning line after line, fact-finding. The baobab tree was turning into the most interesting thing that, until today, we'd known nothing about.

Mom, like a regular parent-spy, curiously peeped at the screen. Seeing a picture of a tree, she sighed and headed back to the kitchen. "You staying for dinner, Quincy? I'm making turkey burgers."

"Sure . . . I mean, what day is this?" he asked me.

"Saturday," I reminded him.

He glanced at the clock, grabbed his backpack, declared, "Oh no, I gotta go!" and dashed to the door. "It's my auntie's birthday. They're having a party at a fancy restaurant. Bye, Miz Reindeer!" he hollered. "Later, Zoe!" The door slammed shut and he was gone.

And minutes later, when Harper reappeared, I'd not only shut off the computer but cleared my browsing history.

Again, I dashed to my room, dug out the pages I'd printed, and pored over the articles. That was when I learned why it's called the tree of life. It gives not only water but also food, plus some people actually live inside of them. I inspected a picture of the pub someone had built inside a six-thousand-year-old baobab.

Reading on, I learned that the trunk can hold huge amounts of water, and that's why the tree can survive when there's a drought, and its fruit, named monkey bread, has healthy vitamins. I thought back to the man who'd come into the nursery this morning and how he'd called it the monkey bread tree. And I was picturing him standing so tall in his two-toned shoes when Mom yelled out, "Dinner!"

Quickly, I stashed the papers under my mattress. If I was going to succeed, this had to remain a secret.

Jade, Harper, and Mom were seated at the table, but only the queen bee was already filling her food hole.

"You're supposed to wait for everyone before you start eating—that's the rule." I glanced at Mom. Please back me up, I thought.

"It is the rule, Jade," Mom told her.

Jade rudely clicked her tongue, turned to me as I sat down, and replied, "Okay, little miz princess of manners."

"BQ, Jade," I replied.

"BQ? What's that supposed to mean?" Jade asked.

"Means 'be quiet,'" I answered.

"That's enough," Mom fussed.

Jade clicked her tongue again. I'd finished one turkey burger and was slathering mustard and ketchup on another when Daddy opened the kitchen door.

"Howdeedoo, family," he said. That's his way, saying *howdeedoo*.

"Hi, Daddy," we said simultaneously.

Mom lifted her head and they gave each other a quick smooch.

"Did you get your *endangered* plants?" I asked, emphasizing the word *endangered*.

Daddy smiled. "Yes," he answered, then washed his hands, sat down at the table, grabbed a handful of fries, and stuffed them in his mouth.

Daddy Reindeer is not as tall as the man from Madagascar, but he's pretty tall, and like me, he wears glasses. When he smiles, his whole face—a face almost as round as a full moon—joins in, especially his eyes. He doesn't like to wear belts, so unless it's some kind of extremely fancy party, he wears suspenders.

Later, I hoped to catch him alone to find out what he knew about baobab trees. I couldn't wait and it was hard to keep from blabbing it right then and there. I smiled inside and out. In fact, for the first time in a while, I had good feelings colliding around inside me, small secret sparks of happiness. It had been eons since I'd had something that felt like it belonged only to me.

After I helped with the dishes, I found a spot on the floor in front of the TV. Every now and then, Mom or

Daddy would act like they were going to bed, but they stayed snuggled together on the sofa until after eleven o'clock. They were in their we're-not-budging-for-a-while comfortable pose, which led me to the sad conclusion that I probably wasn't going to get a chance to talk to Daddy tonight after all.

That being the case, I said, "G'night."

I showered and was about to climb into bed when I decided to give it one more try. Finally, I found him alone at his desk, sorting through the mail.

"Daddy?"

"Howdeedoo, Zoe."

I leaned against the desk. "A man came into the nursery while you were gone, and he asked—"

"Asked about buying this property again?"

I was about to say no, but Daddy started ranting loudly. "If any more land developers come in here asking one more time to buy this property so they can build town houses or apartments or condominiums, you tell them I said I'm not selling! You hear me, Zoe? Tell them I'm not selling now. In fact . . . tell them I'm not selling . . . ever!"

"But . . ."

"Is that all, Zoe? Because I've got all these bills to take care of." He frowned and waved one at me. Lately he seemed worried about money, and more and more, I'd heard him and Mom arguing about the bills. "G'night, Zoe."

He'll be in a better mood tomorrow, I figured. Then I'll talk to him about baobab trees and tell him what I've found out. I snuggled his shoulder, said, "G'night, Daddy," and trudged to my room.

Disappointed and feeling a little gloomy, I started thinking. This whole Zoe-saves-the-baobabs idea was ridiculous. I was more than likely never going to do anything special or be anyone special.

But the next thought that climbed into my mind changed me from a teeny sad sack to an enormous elephant-size worrywart.

I remembered Quincy telling me that the reason his parents got a divorce, or "went *splitsville*," as he calls it, was because there never seemed to be enough money and they were always fighting about it. Suddenly, I got terrified. More than anything, I didn't want my mom and daddy to ever go *splitsville*.

Then another worry plopped on top of that one. What if Daddy changed his mind and sold the Wonderland? I didn't want to live anywhere but here.

These two worries brought every spark of happiness that had been dancing around inside me to a slow stop.

The moon lit my room through the half-open slats

of my window's shutters. Outside, an army of crickets chirped.

This had been a day of strange happenings—the astronomer from Madagascar and baobab trees. The beautiful picture of the row of baobabs flashed in my mind. I wanted to see one of the huge trees in person, but I doubted that would ever happen. Madagascar was a long way away.

I peeked out at the globe in the dark sky and for a few seconds wondered whether the tall man had a special name for the moon too. I climbed into bed, thinking about baobabs and the moon.

But it was the two worries that kept me staring at the ceiling, unable to fall asleep.

10

Now Open on Sunday

The following day, Daddy didn't go to church with us. Instead, he opened the Wonderland. For as long as I could remember, the Wonderland had always been closed on Sundays.

"It's because of all the bills, huh?" I asked Mom as we drove.

Mom stared straight ahead. "I may be going back to school to get my teaching credentials. With another degree I'd make more money."

She'd been talking about going back to school for years, but so far that's all it's been—talk.

"We could sell it," Jade said.

"Sell what?" Mom asked.

"The Weirdland. I mean, if it's not making enough money, what's the point? It's a stupid place to live, anyway. If we sell it, we can live somewhere normal," Jade answered.

"It's not called the Weirdland," I reminded her again.

"I'll call it whatever I want to call it!" Jade informed me in her snippy way.

Mom spoke up. "We are not selling the Wonderland. It's your daddy's life."

Jade kept yapping, "I'm just saying . . ."

Mom frowned. "Not another word, Miss."

Miss was code for "if you have good sense, you'll shut up now." And Jade did.

When we got home, I found Daddy trimming his bonsai trees and plants. He was whistling a tune the way he sometimes does when he's happily working. The sound of his whistling always makes me smile. Over and over, from the time I was little, I'd tried to learn how, putting my lips together and blowing. But no matter what, I'd only been able to produce the sound of plain old air, and after I'd failed for what felt like the hundredth time, I'd finally given up.

"Howdeedoo, Zoe," he said when he saw me.

There were no customers around that I could see and I wondered if any had come in. "Any business?" I asked.

"Not yet," he replied without looking up. "Suppose folks in the neighborhood are used to us being closed on Sundays."

"You could put a sign outside that says 'Now Open on Sundays.' Then people would know," I said.

He looked up at me and smiled. "Good idea, Zoe . . . very good idea."

Right then, inside Zoe G. Reindeer, a spark or two of happiness came to life.

And because I finally had his attention, it seemed like a perfect time to bring up baobab trees. "By the way, Daddy, that man from yesterday wasn't trying to buy the Wonderland. He was from Madagascar and he was looking for baobab trees, but Grandpa checked the computer and said we don't have any. Do we?"

"Baobab? That tree that looks upside down?"

"Uh-huh," I answered. "Some people even call it the upside-down tree and the monkey bread tree."

"Monkey bread tree?" He completely stopped what he was doing. "That, I didn't know."

I blurted out the other stuff I knew about baobabs and ended with, "It's endangered."

"Endangered, huh?" he repeated, and went back to working on his miniature tree. "Didn't know that either."

Now, I thought. "If it's endangered, shouldn't we buy some?" I asked.

"Very hard to grow in this climate, Zoe. That much I do know. Temperatures in Pasadena can dip to near freezing some winters."

"Maybe we could buy one and try to grow it in the greenhouse. I'd take care of it."

Daddy sighed. "Not now, Zoe. The cacti I bought yesterday cost me more than I thought, plus the gas to get to the desert and back, and the other bills . . . Not now, Zoe."

Like a rock tossed in the pond, my spirits sank. "Okay," I replied.

"But the sign's a good idea. I'll get to work on that as soon as I'm finished here," he added.

"I could help you," I offered.

"And let your mom catch you working on a Sunday? You know how she is . . . bad enough me being out here."

He was right. I'd heard Mom warning him earlier this morning that everyone needed a day of rest and ours was supposed to be Sunday.

"Well, can you at least teach me how to trim the bonsai? That's not working—it's learning." I'd asked him I don't know how many times before, but he'd always said no, I wasn't old enough.

A smile painted his face and loud laughter flew

from his mouth. Daddy motioned me to come close. "Okay, Zoe."

Right then, *Imaginary Zoe* knocked on the door to my mind.

It was Zoe's graduation day from college. Of course, Zoe looked gorgeous in her black cap and gown. She received degrees in both horticulture and business. Daddy and Mom presented her with a bouquet of flowers. One day soon, she'd expand the family business. She'd change the name to Zoe's Exotic Plant Wonderland and have locations all over the country.

"Zoe?" Daddy said.

"Huh?"

"Daydreaming again?"

I didn't know he'd noticed. "Kinda," I replied.

He placed my hand around the small pruning clippers. "This requires precision, Zoe. Very carefully, clip right here." He pointed to a spot. "But be careful."

I squeezed and clipped. A teeny piece of leaf fell off. My hands were a little shaky and beads of sweat broke out on my face.

"Very good!" he said, and pointed to another spot. "Now here."

I was ready to clip again when my glasses slipped down and I missed, cutting off an entire tiny branch instead.

"Zoe!" he fussed, then yanked the clippers from my hand.

"Sorry. My glasses slipped—I couldn't see. It's not my fault, Daddy. Really."

Sometimes I can't do anything right.

"Sorry," I repeated. "Don't be mad."

Daddy patted my hand. "I'm not mad, Zoe. We all make mistakes."

It was feeling like one of those times when he was going to say "I love you," but a woman customer walked through the door and grabbed his attention.

"Okay if I go to Quincy's?" I asked.

Daddy glanced at the wall clock. "Yes, but be sure and be back by five. We're having dinner at your nana's."

"I will," I replied. And while he waited on the lady, who was the first customer to discover we were now open on Sundays, Zoe G. Reindeer slipped outside.

11

The Movie

As usual, our next-door neighbor Mrs. Warner was outside, rearranging her *creatures*, as she calls them—mostly small statues and gnomes and stuff. From what I've seen, nothing ever gets added or subtracted, just moved from place to place. Supposedly, she's more than a hundred years old, and Daddy says the inside of her house has so many piled-up newspapers and magazines that he doesn't understand how anyone can live in there. Daddy claims it's like a maze. And because I like mazes, I'm curious to get inside, but she's never invited me. The only thing that separates her house from ours is a low wooden fence, and because my bedroom is closest to that fence, some nights the flickering lights from her candles dance on my walls and her old-time jazz music helps puts me to sleep.

Mrs. Warner, who has a very bad memory, said in her raspy voice, "How're you, little Miss Jade?"

"I'm not Jade, I'm Zoe," I reminded her for what seemed like the thousandth time.

"It's so nice to see you on this beautiful day, little Miss Jade." She smiled.

Some days her memory was normal and she made sense. Other times it was useless, like today.

She squatted, brushed a space in the dirt with her hand, and put down the statue. "You have a nice day now, little Miss Jade."

I reached for her hand and patted it gently. "You too, Mrs. Warner."

I felt sad as I walked away. No one ever came to her house except for the people from the senior-meals place or the van that takes people to the doctor. "Bye," I told her, and headed to Quincy's.

On the way, I tried very hard to push baobab trees out of my head. Even if we did have the money, it's a dumb idea, I convinced myself.

I rang Quincy's bell.

"Who is it?" his mom, Kendra, hollered from inside.

"*Just* Zoe!" I answered.

"Door's open!"

I turned the knob and stepped inside.

Normally on Sunday—Kendra's only day off from work—you'd find her sprawled on the sofa with the TV remote glued to her hand. Instead, she was in the kitchen doing something I had hardly ever seen her do before—cooking. Her hair was pulled back into a ponytail. He eyes were red and watery, like she'd been crying.

"You okay, Miz Hill?" I asked.

Kendra, short and curvy, gazed at me with her hazel eyes, pointed to the onions she was chopping, and smiled. "Onions," she replied. Then, she stopped cooking, wiped her hands on a dish towel, stepped toward me, and stretched out her arms. "Gimme a hug, girl. You know my rule. You can't come in this house and not give Kendra a hug. Give it here . . . and make it a good one." Kendra cooking was unusual, but Kendra hugging was not. She swallowed me up in her arms and I hugged her back.

Every now and then, I find myself wishing my mom were more like Kendra—the hugging stuff, anyway.

She motioned toward their den. "He's in there, on the computer probably."

Quincy and I bumped into each other in the hallway.

"I found out a lot more stuff about baobab trees,"

Quincy said as we settled in front of his computer. "The bark is even used for making ropes, but the reason they're endangered is because people have been cutting them down because they want the land to grow other stuff or they need places for their herds to graze." Quincy took a deep breath and rattled on, "But the most interesting thing is that the fruit isn't pollinated by bees; it's pollinated by fruit bats. Interesting, huh?"

I wanted to tell him to BQ, *be quiet*, but instead I just shrugged.

"Whatsamatter, Zoe?"

"My daddy said no." And instead of telling him about the bills and stuff, I added, "He's heard of them, but he said he has enough plants for now."

"But I had this idea for an amazing movie."

Movie ideas were like vitamins to Quincy. He usually had one a day.

"What kind of movie now?" I asked.

"I thought we could buy some baobab seeds, which aren't that expensive, maybe five dollars online, and I would make a movie from planting them and then videotaping them as they grow week by week, until you finally give them to your dad. I'm calling it *Zoe and the Baobabs*."

"Hmmm? I didn't even think about seeds," I told him.

"We can buy them online."

I flicked his shoulder. "With what? We need a credit card, genius."

"We could ask my mom. She's been nicer than ever lately, so I don't think she'll say no. It's not that much money, anyway." He bolted to the living room and returned in no time at all with Kendra. "See, told you."

"Is this for a school project?" she asked.

"A movie," he answered. "I'm going to make a video of everything from when we plant the seeds to when they start to grow, and turn it into a movie."

"My baby, the director." Kendra smiled and kissed the top of Quincy's head. "Are you two hungry?" she asked. "Because I'm going to have a four-course meal ready soon."

"I'll just have a little because I'm having Sunday dinner at my nana's."

Once she'd left, he said, "My mom's been off from work all week on vacation and cooking every day. It's weird. Except for dessert, it mostly doesn't taste that good, but I don't want to hurt her feelings, so I've been eating and eating. I'll be glad when she goes back to work and starts bringing home takeout again."

Then he grabbed his video camera, pointed it at me, and began recording. "It's October in Pasadena, California. We just bought the baobab seeds online, and this is Zoe G. Reindeer," he said. "Smile, Zoe," he directed.

I smiled, but it must have looked fake.

"Again, Zoe . . . like you mean it," Quincy commanded.

I grinned from ear to ear.

"That's more like it!"

12

Waiting

I really hate waiting. I hate waiting every day for at least a gazillion minutes for Jade to get out of the bathroom. I hate waiting in any kind of line, especially in the cafeteria, especially when I finally get to the food and the very thing I got in line for in the first place—the mac and cheese—is gone.

Now I had something else to wait for—baobab seeds. It'd been three days.

The school-is-finally-over-for-the-day bell rang.

"Do you think they came today?" I asked as I tagged along beside Quincy after school.

"Dunno," he replied. "Let's go see."

"I've been thinking we should grow them at your

house. That way, I can really surprise my daddy. Do you think your mom would let you . . . in the garage?"

"I spoze. Not like she parks her car there or anything. But I thought you said they'd need a special light or something."

"I'm going to sneak one out of the greenhouse. He has some that he hardly ever uses. I have everything we need, including potting soil," I informed him.

"Plus it'd be easier to make the movie," he agreed.

"And the only way to keep the snox out of our business."

❧

Another day passed, and another. It was just about dinnertime on Friday evening when our doorbell rang. "Zoe? Quincy's here!" Mom called out.

As usual, he had shown up unannounced. He was standing in the doorway, holding a small package, grinning.

I joined him on the porch, closing the door behind me, and we huddled together.

"Got 'em," he whispered.

We looked at the seeds, which sort of looked like black beans, and made a pact to meet at his house tomorrow to plant them and start the movie. Quincy was making a joke about Jack and the Beanstalk when the door creaked open and the snox peeked out. He was wearing a plaid fedora.

"What're you guys doing?" Harper asked, and put one foot outside.

In a flash, Quincy stashed the seeds in his jacket pocket.

"We're doing nunya business, nosy," I answered.

Harper squinted at us, but Quincy stared him down with his best I-am-a-bigger-boy-man-than-you look, which made the snox slink back into the house and shut the door.

Quincy laughed. "See you tomorrow, Zoe," he said, and turned to walk away.

"Tomorrow," I echoed, and crept inside.

13

A Super-Sad Saturday

After I finished up in the greenhouse the next day, I gathered the light, potting soil, and some old coffee cans (which Nana used to collect and are kind of cool to grow things in), put everything in a wheelbarrow, and rolled it to Quincy's house.

To my surprise, his dad opened the door. Even though his body is slim, his cheeks are fat and he always reminds me of a teddy bear. I hadn't seen him since Quincy's birthday party in the summer. He gave me an arm hug and squealed my name just like always: "Zo-eeee, long time no see." He smiled, but his eyes looked sad, and I supposed he didn't like being divorced.

"Hi, Wes," I said.

Noticing the wheelbarrow, he asked, "What you got there?"

"We're going to plant some seeds and make a movie out of it," I informed him as I came inside.

"An Academy Award winner, I bet."

I shrugged my shoulders. "I don't think so. We're just kids."

"Yeah, just kids," he repeated, then settled on the sofa in front of the television the way he used to when he lived there. But instead of turning on the TV, Wes rested his head in his hands and stared at the floor. I looked around for Kendra but didn't see her. Two big suitcases sat on the floor near the front door.

I figured Quincy would be happy—the way he usually is when his dad's around—but when he came into the room, he had a strange look, as if someone had stolen every bit of his happiness, even the crumbs. His eyes were red like he'd been crying. He butted the front screen door open with his hand in a mad way and headed outside.

I followed. "Whatsamatter?"

He shrugged.

"Why's your dad here?" I asked.

"Because," he replied.

"Is he staying?"

"Definitely not. He finally got a new job a couple of months ago, a real good one in San Francisco."

I didn't know what was wrong, but I figured he'd tell me sooner or later. I pointed toward the wheelbarrow. "I brought all the stuff to plant the baobab seeds."

Quincy got a worse-than-not-happy look. "You're going to have to plant them at your house," he told me.

"We can't because my dad will find them and it's supposed to be a secret," I reminded him.

"But I'm leaving," Quincy said sadly.

"Leaving where?"

"Here . . . to go live with my dad . . . for now, anyway."

"What!" I screeched. "All the way in San Francisco? . . . No way . . . You can't leave me!" I tugged on his shirt.

"I have to. My mom is sick."

"But I just saw her and she didn't look sick to me."

"She is. She has cancer. She had surgery early this morning."

I had to sit down. "How come you didn't tell me?" I asked.

"My dad just told me a little while ago. She has to have some treatments to kill the rest of the cancer. She'll be at a special hospital for at least six weeks. So they decided that I should go live with my dad until she's all better."

"How long will it take for her to get better?"

"Who knows?"

Quincy pulled the packet of baobab seeds from his pocket and dropped it in my hand. "I have to go to the hospital now," he said. I'd never seen him cry. I can't even remember ever seeing his eyes water, but right then his eyes filled up with tears.

Some tears, like some diseases, are very contagious. A bunch of them got in my eyes too. "Sorry about your mom," I told him.

"Yeah, me too. Now I know why she was doing all that fancy cooking and being extra-special nice."

For a while, there was a lot of not-talking and looking at each other, and then I glanced away and then we stared at each other again, both of us fighting more tears. I rubbed his arm gently and he took my hand and—for the first time ever—held it, but only for a few seconds.

Quincy's dad lugged the suitcases outside, locked the front door, and gave me another shoulder hug. "You two can lose the worried looks. Kendra's got too much fight in her to lose any battle. Heck, Kendra could win a war against aliens from outer space."

Finally, Quincy smiled.

Mr. Hill loaded the suitcases, slammed the trunk closed, got in, and started the car. "Time to go, buddy. Later now, Zoe."

Quincy climbed in the car and stared at the seed pack in my hand. "Swear you'll plant them and e-mail me pictures."

"I swear," I told him.

"Okay. Bye, Zoe."

"Bye." I waved.

Quincy twisted around in his seat, and I could see him through the car's rear window waving back. I stood there as motionless as a mannequin, watching until their car vanished from sight and then watching some more—part of me thinking maybe I was dreaming, but the majority of me knowing I wasn't.

Slowly, I rolled the wheelbarrow toward home, trying my best to keep the tears from trickling, but they won by finding another way out through my nose. I wiped at it with my sleeve.

14

The Worst Zoe Mood Ever

Mrs. Warner was outside in her yard, fiddling around with her statues. I didn't want to talk to anyone and hoped she would ignore me. But, of course, she didn't. "Having a nice day, little Miss Jade?"

I pretended not to hear her. My sadness made it impossible to be polite, even to a forgetful old lady.

"You hear me, Miss Jade?"

Zoe G. Reindeer was in a stinking mood, possibly her worst mood ever. This was a day of extremely sad news. No one should bother anyone on a day of extremely sad news.

"Little Miss Jade?" she repeated.

Instantly, my sad stuff transformed itself into mad

stuff. "I'm not little Miss Jade! I'm Zoe! Stop calling me Jade!" I snapped.

Mrs. Warner stared at me like she was seeing me for the first time ever and responded, "That's right . . . You're the one with those big feet you're always tripping over." She placed her hand over her mouth, trying to hold in the giggle, but it still came out.

Trying desperately not to yell at her again, I clenched my jaw.

But she kept on talking. "If you're fortunate, you might grow into those big feet. Tall, I mean."

I didn't want it to, but my bad temper won. "BQ!" I hollered.

"BQ?" she asked. "Who's BQ?"

I huffed at her. Then, to keep something I'd really be sorry for from coming out of my mouth, I pursed my lips and continued guiding the wheelbarrow toward the Wonderland.

The only thing I really wanted to do was go to my room, shut the door, and be very alone. But because I knew that if I didn't plant them now, I probably never would, I headed to the greenhouse to plant the baobab seeds. I had to keep my promise to my best and only friend. And if Daddy asks what I'm growing, I decided, I'll just tell him it's a surprise.

There were some directions, but I ignored them. I

really wasn't in the mood. After all, a seed is a seed. You give it dirt and water and it grows. I planted all four seeds, one in each of Nana's old coffee cans. One label said Royal Kona Hawaiian Coffee, one said Hills Bros., another had a Chock full o'Nuts label, and the last one was in a Folgers can. I watered them and tucked them in a corner of the greenhouse.

Leaning against one of the shelves, I started thinking. Why do adults think that it's okay to keep humongous secrets from kids—secrets bigger than an eight-ton Tyrannosaurus rex? If my mom or daddy were very sick, I sure wouldn't want to be the last to know.

Slowly, I sank to the dirt floor and pulled my knees to my chest. I was feeling extremely miserable about Kendra, hoping she wouldn't die, and now I was nervous about whether my mom and daddy were keeping sad secrets too. And what if Quincy never came back?

Despite the quiet of the greenhouse, the question sounded loud inside my head. "Maybe I'll never see him again," I whimpered.

Suddenly, from out of nowhere, Harper spoke. "See who?" he asked. "And who are you talking to?" he added.

Please! Please! Please! Not now! Plus, the greenhouse is my special place.

I glared at my brother. He was wearing a straw cowboy hat and, as usual, a smirk.

How did he sneak in here without me hearing him?

Like a volcano, I exploded. "Get out! Leave me alone! You're driving me crazy!" I shot up from the floor and lunged at him.

I must have really looked crazy-mad, because Harper's eyes were filled with fright and he took off running. He pushed the greenhouse door open and bolted. I chased him, but I'm nowhere near as fast as Harper.

And then—I tripped and fell, landing hard on the flagstone. Instantly, my knees burned and I knew they were scraped up bad. My jeans were torn and blood oozed.

I panted until, like water down a drain, my madness disappeared.

At first, Daddy grinned as I made my into the Wonderland's store. Fortunately, he was alone. "Howdee-doo, Zoe," he said. Then, noticing my bloody knees, he asked, "What happened?"

I zoomed to him, hugged his waist, sank my face in his shirt, and sobbed.

15

Not Just Zoe Tonight

Gently, Mom cleaned my knees and put medicine and Band-Aids on them while Daddy found out what hospital Kendra was in and arranged for a room full of flowers—mostly orchids, her favorites—to be delivered to her.

My mom called the hospital and actually talked to Kendra on the phone and made plans for us to visit her early tomorrow before she got transferred to the special cancer treatment hospital that's far away for chemotherapy and radiation.

At dinner that night, Harper and Jade were forced not to be mean to me. I didn't even have to help with dishes.

And later, before I went to sleep, Mom and Daddy

both came in my room. Mom sat on my bed, and Daddy plopped into my beanbag chair. For the first time in a long time, I had them totally to myself and that felt kind of awesome.

"It's a type of cancer with a high cure rate," Mom said.

"That means she'll get all better?" I asked.

Mom patted my hand. "I hope so, Zoe."

"Quincy could have stayed here with us, if I'd known," Daddy said.

I lit up. "Are you serious? Because maybe we can call his dad and he could bring him back and then he can still go to school here and—"

Daddy interrupted me. "Calm down, Zoe. I was just thinking out loud. This is family business . . . their family business."

"Besides, he'll probably be home before you know it," Mom added, which got me thinking maybe she knew something I didn't. Possibly there was another secret.

I sat up in bed and asked, "Why do grown-ups think that it's okay to keep secrets from kids?"

"To protect them," Daddy replied.

It was exactly the answer I'd expected. "But it's not fair to lie to us," I told them.

This time, Mom answered. "It's not lying."

I disagreed. "Seems like it to me."

"It's keeping the truth in, Zoe. Because sometimes the truth is hard," Daddy explained.

"Or sometimes we do it to keep kids from worrying too much," Mom added.

"But when we finally find out, we still worry. Plus, if Quincy had known that his mom was sick, he could have been really nice to her, the same way she was being really nice to him. And I could have given her flowers before she went to the hospital instead of after. And that would have made her happy because she's always saying how she loves orchids but they cost too much."

I suppose they thought we had reached the end of our parent-Zoe talk, because they both kissed me and said good night.

But I still had more questions. "How come some people get really sick?" I asked.

Daddy thought for a while before answering. "Human beings can be fragile creatures, fragile the way some flowers are." He paused briefly, then added, "Some things are hard to understand when you're young."

"Some things are hard to understand, period," Mom said.

"Before you go, I have one more question," I told them.

Daddy sighed. "Hope we have the answer, Zoe."

"Do you guys have any important sad secrets I should know?"

"No, Zoe," they said at the same time. "G'night, Zoe."

"G'night," I said.

"Want us to leave your door open?" Mom asked.

"I'm not a baby."

"Love you," they said softly.

"Love you too."

I lay there wondering what Quincy was doing and if he'd gotten to San Francisco yet. It hadn't even been a whole day, but I already missed him, and even though I supposed he was mostly worried about his mom, I secretly hoped he was at least a little lonesome for me. Being lonely for him tasted like something sour. And worrying about Kendra tasted even worse.

For the first day in a very long time, *Imaginary Zoe* stayed completely away. Being so super-smart, she must have known it's better to be quiet on a day of too much extremely sad news.

I pulled the comforter up around my neck and watched the lights from Mrs. Warner's candles dance across the walls of my room.

16

The Hospital and Kendra

On the entire day and night of too much extremely sad news, *Imaginary Zoe* seemed to have vanished, but on the drive to the hospital, she suddenly reappeared.

> *Zoe was holding a pot of gold coins. She was at a place called the New People Store, where people could be duplicated. And if someone you loved died, you just headed to the New People Store and shopped for another one just like him or her—same personality and everything. If Kendra didn't get well, Zoe knew exactly where to go.*

Before I knew it, Daddy was parking the car in the hospital's lot, and a short time later the automatic doors parted in front of us. After getting our visitor passes, Daddy, Mom, and I walked along the clean gleaming floors of the extraordinarily long hallway toward Kendra's room.

Three Things About Hospitals

1. Hospitals are like toilet paper. We don't really think about them much until we need them.
2. Like ice rinks, hospitals are always cold.
3. And the same way a mechanic can usually fix your car but other times can't, sometimes being in the hospital fixes people and other times, no matter what, it doesn't.

Kendra's room looked like there'd been an explosion of flowers.

She was propped up in bed, sleeping. Some tubes were hooked up to her arms and her head was shaved bald.

Why is her head shaved? I wondered.

Daddy put his finger to his mouth, whispered, "Shhh," and we turned to leave.

But right then, Kendra woke up. "Zoe?"

I smiled. "Hi."

"Gimme a hug," she commanded.

So I did. But I must have hugged her too tight, because she groaned a little.

"Sorry!" I told her.

Kendra reached for my hands and held them. "Sorries aren't allowed here, Zoe dear."

I wanted to inform her that she'd just made a rhyme but didn't.

"We won't stay long," Mom told her.

"You need your rest," Daddy added.

"Thank you for the flowers, Doc and Gabby. Never had so many . . . ever." Kendra glanced out the window, and I could tell she was trying hard not to cry. She won the battle with her tears after a minute, and then she smiled. Remembering how Quincy's dad had called her a fighter, I pictured Kendra kickboxing, defeating the cancer.

We were still talking when some of Kendra's family showed up and stuck their heads in the door. Because the hospital had a limit on the number of visitors a person can have inside their room, we said our goodbyes and left.

"Why'd they shave her hair off?" I asked on the drive home.

"They didn't. Kendra did that herself," Mom replied.

"Said the chemo and radiation were going to make her hair fall out, anyway. That's sometimes hard on a person. So she decided to save herself from that."

"She still looks pretty. Even without any hair. Don't you think?" I told her.

"She does," Mom answered.

From the backseat, I gazed at the city's scenery and cars as they zoomed by, thought about Kendra, and wondered if there would ever really be a place like the New People Store.

17

Without Quincy

Two Things Being Without Quincy Was Like

1. Being barefoot and stepping in dog poop.
2. The worst, most boring Zoe days ever.

If my world with Quincy had been, for instance, the size of Catalina Island, my world without him was now the size of an extremely small iceberg—an iceberg that was only big enough for one person to stand on: me. And my happy feelings, like an iceberg, were frozen. Secretly, I vowed not to smile again until Quincy returned and Kendra got better.

At school, I spent a lot of time watching the clocks tick the time away. And when the end-of-the-day bell finally rang, I felt the way a prisoner must feel when she gets out of jail on a one-day or weekend pass—unable to feel too good about it because she knows that before very long, she's going to wind up right back where she doesn't want to be.

Almost every other day Quincy called me, and as soon as I'd hear his voice, I couldn't help but smile, temporarily breaking my vow. And we e-mailed each other almost every day, but it was nowhere even close to having him at school or Kendra and him living right up the street. Plus I really missed our not-a-date Saturdays at the movies.

At home, I did my best to be alone.

"She'll get over it," I'd heard Daddy tell Mom.

"Soon, I hope," she'd replied.

They made it sound like the flu.

The Reindeer parents have a rule about no cell phones until you're twelve. But because I knew they felt sorry for me, I thought maybe they might make an exception. Parent pity just might work in my favor. "Can I please get a cell phone?" I'd begged at dinner. "That way, Quincy and I can text each other." I glanced from Daddy to Mom, hoping at least one of them would weaken, but they remained parent-allies.

Not even pity could make them break their cell-phone rule.

"Can I use yours sometimes?" I'd asked Jade.

Jade cracked up laughing. "You can't be serious. As if . . ."

The only thing that really changed at the Wonderland was Daddy taught me how to use the register. But mostly it wasn't teaching because I already knew from watching him and Grandpa all this time. It was pretty easy, and after a while he started letting me ring stuff up for customers and even count out the change.

And that's where I was when the tall man from Madagascar came back to the Wonderland. Because it was a warm day, the door was propped wide open. Quietly, he ducked inside. The T-shirt he wore had the word CURIOSITY printed on it.

Just like before, it was a Saturday morning, and also just like before, Daddy wasn't there. This time, he'd gone to a plant show at the botanical gardens in Arcadia. But unlike before, Grandpa Reindeer was outside, asleep in the hammock, one leg dangling off, the book he'd been reading resting on his chest.

The tall man smiled, showing both his top and bottom teeth. "Hello again, young lady."

Young lady is not a name, I thought. "Zoe," I informed him.

"Hello, Zoe. I'm Ben . . . Ben Rakotomalala."

I'd never heard a last name like that before. I tried to pronounce it but couldn't. "Rakoto . . . huh?"

"Rakotomalala," he repeated. "Actually one of the shorter names in Madagascar and quite common. Most people call me Ben."

Seeing him again made me instantly un-forget about the baobabs. Since the day I'd planted the seeds, I'd completely ignored them. They hadn't even been watered. And Quincy hadn't reminded me. I suppose both of our minds had been on other things. As soon as the man leaves, I promised myself, I'll head to the greenhouse.

"We still don't have any baobab trees," I told him. "And I asked my daddy, but he didn't want to buy any, so my friend and I bought some seeds and I planted them, so we should have some pretty soon, maybe."

My Zoe shyness is never completely gone. Sometimes, like lint in the dryer, there's a huge wad of it, and other times, there's only enough to make a small ball of lint fluff. Right now, probably because I liked the tall man, there was only a little fluff.

"So Zoe is an entrepreneur?"

I didn't know what an entrepreneur was, but I felt ashamed to ask, so I just shrugged. "Spoze so?"

"Didn't see you at the open house we had at JPL last week."

"Oh. I forgot all about it, plus I'm not really into science. My brother, Harper, he's the scientist. He knows a whole bunch of stuff."

"But you're the imaginer?"

Because he was right, I nodded.

"Imagination is sometimes more valuable than having a head full of facts. Without imaginers, it's likely we'd still be living in caves. Imaginers and adventurers can change the world."

"But I'm not an adventurer," I told him.

"I'll be right back. I have something for you!" he exclaimed as he dashed outside.

Through the open door, I peeked as he rummaged through his car's trunk. On the back of his T-shirt was a picture of a telescope. "Rakotomalala," I whispered.

Seconds later, he slammed the trunk closed, and quickly, his long-as-stilts legs brought him back to where I was standing. He was holding a book. He handed it to me. "A small gift for you."

Because the Reindeer parents had taught us not to accept things from strangers, at first I was reluctant to take it. But it was only a book, and a paperback, even. I took it from his hand and read the title. *Adventurers,*

Explorers, Inventors, Dreamers, and Imaginers: People Who Changed Our World.

"I hope this will open your mind, Zoe," he said. "And that your life will be a marvelous adventure," he added.

I glanced at the cover of the book and then back at the tall man from Madagascar named Ben Rakotoma-lala. "Thank you."

"You are very welcome, Zoe. Time for me to go." Before he ducked outside, he told me, "Promise you'll save one for me."

"One what?"

"Baobab."

"I promise."

"So long for now, Zoe."

"So long," I said, but I suddenly remembered the question I'd had about the moon. I rushed to the door. "Ben?"

He halted. "Yes?"

"Is there a special name for the moon . . . like you have for the sun?"

He smiled and replied, "No, we astronomers just call it the Moon, but we spell it with a capital *M*, and for the record, the official name for the star of day is the Sun. I prefer *star of day* because it sounds poetic. Don't you agree?"

"Yes."

"Enjoy the book, Zoe Reindeer."

"Thank you. I will."

I stared at the picture of the telescope on the back of his T-shirt as he walked away and wondered exactly how far away you can see with one.

Just like before, his tailpipe sputtered as he drove off. I studied the cover of the book again, then gazed up at the sky.

18

Trouble

Instead of listening to the teacher, I was busy reading the book Ben had given me. Since Saturday, I couldn't keep my nose out of it. There were so many stories about people who everyone called dreamers—

Zoe had navigated the spacecraft to the planet of a distant galaxy. As captain, she landed the ship safely and her loyal crew leaped to their feet, cheering. She stepped outside the ship and smiled. It was exactly the way she'd pictured it, with its rivers and green hillsides and pastures where huge flowers and baobab trees grew.

"Are you daydreaming, Zoe?" a voice asked. I glanced up. My teacher, Mr. Summer, was standing over me.

Startled, I said the first thing that came to my mind—the truth. "Yes," I answered.

A few of the girls laughed.

My face got hot with embarrassment.

"Maybe you'd like to share with the class what you were daydreaming about?" Mr. Summer said.

"No, thank you. I don't think so."

Zena, a queen-bee mean girl who was sitting behind me, declared, "Probably dreaming about her *boy-friend,* Quincy, coming back."

This time, it seemed like the entire class cracked up. "Settle down!" Mr. Summer commanded.

Zena was occasionally mean to me, but now, with Quincy gone, she was making snide remarks more and more. Quincy called her clique of friends "Zena's puppets." I turned around to face her. "He's my best friend, not my boyfriend."

Of course, Zena mocked me, repeating my words in her whiny voice, and the kids nearby who heard her chuckled again. And that made her keep it up. "I know that's right," she added, "because Quincy could sure do a whole lot better than Zoe the *so-not-cute* Reindeer girl—U-G-L-Y," Zena spelled out.

Snickering followed, filling the room, and fingers, mostly from Zena and her puppets, pointed my way.

"Settle down!" Mr. Summer commanded again.

But Zena ignored him, leaned toward me, and said, "Zoe, the U-G-L-Y Reindeer girl."

This time, Mr. Summer must have heard exactly what she said. "That's enough, Zena!" he scolded. "Bullying and name-calling will not be tolerated."

But it was too late to save my feelings, and the same way Jade used to make me so mad that I'd cry, I knew tears were going to be coming.

No way was Zena ever going to see me cry.

I grabbed the book Ben had given me, shoved it in my backpack, and ran to the door. But before I ran out, I turned to Zena and blurted, "BQ! BQ! BQ!" Tears began rolling down my cheeks as I bolted down the hall toward the exit doors.

"Zoe!" Mr. Summer yelled.

But I didn't stop. I didn't even look back. I kept running, and for some reason, I didn't trip over my feet.

"Zoe, come back!" Mr. Summer hollered from behind me, and I could hear him trotting toward me. But Mr. Summer is a little chubby and I knew there was no way he could catch me.

I burst outside through the doors and sprinted.

Soon, I was around the corner. I kept running for almost three blocks, until I was almost out of breath. Now what? I thought. There was a bus stop two blocks away. I had fifteen dollars in my wallet and my bus pass.

And so I got on the bus to Old Pasadena and went to the movies and read subtitles and ate popcorn and drank soda and pretended Quincy was right there beside me. And when the movie was over, I walked up and down Colorado Boulevard, looking in the shops until it was way past time for school to be out, but when I stopped to get an ice cream cone, I discovered I didn't have enough money left. So I headed to the bus stop and boarded the bus that took me back to the Wonderland.

Mrs. Warner was outside in her yard, sitting on the ground with her legs sprawled out in front of her. "I fell. Can you help me up?"

"Are you okay?" I asked as I quickly opened her chain-link gate and hurried toward her.

"I'm fine . . . just lost my balance."

I reached for her hands and pulled her to her feet. Luckily, Mrs. Warner didn't weigh much and it was easy. "Are you sure you didn't hurt yourself? Maybe you should go to the doctor."

"And have her threaten to put me in the old-people orphanage again? No, little ma'am. I don't think so," she answered as I helped her hobble over to a chair and sit down.

"Where's your family?" I asked.

She shook her head. "Gone . . . gone . . . all gone."

"Oh," I replied, and reached for my backpack.

Mrs. Warner stared at it hard. "What'd you do, play hooky from school?" she asked.

How'd she know? "Huh?"

"Your mom and daddy came over earlier, asking if I'd seen you. You in some kind of trouble?"

"Probably."

19

Back at the Wonderland

*Four Things That Have Landed
Zoe G. Reindeer in Trouble*

1. Throwing a shoe at Harper, which missed him completely but went through the living room window instead, shattering it. That was last year.
2. Telling my third-grade teacher and class that our entire family had taken a three-month summer vacation all over Europe and Africa, when actually we'd only spent a week at Pismo Beach. That was a couple of years ago.

3. Trying to make doughnuts with Quincy from scratch and winding up with greasy dough plastered on our kitchen walls, cabinets, and ceiling. That was just this past summer.
4. Becoming a truant. That was today.

As quietly as I could, I crept into the Wonderland. A police car was parked in the driveway. Was that for me being a truant? They couldn't put me in jail, could they? If Quincy were here, he'd have the answer.

But I was on my own and I was getting scared and I didn't know what to do. And so, I decided to hide.

I snuck into the greenhouse, slid under one of the tables, used my backpack for a pillow, and put my head down to rest.

୨

"Wake up, Miss!" A bright light was shining in my face. A flashlight. It was nighttime.

It took a few seconds, but my sleepy eyes zeroed in on the policeman's brass badge. Terror got inside of me. My heart pounded fast.

"Are you going to arrest me?" I asked the officer.

"Nope, not going to arrest you, Miss. Are you okay?"

I nodded and crawled out from where I'd been hiding.

The policeman helped me up, looked me in the eyes, and made me promise never to run away again. "You could have become a statistic."

I didn't know what a statistic was, but from the way he'd said it, it didn't sound like something anyone should become, so I promised him.

"Found her!" the policeman yelled.

Suddenly, I was surrounded by other people all pointing flashlights in my direction, including some neighbors, my mom and daddy, Nana and Grandpa, Harper and Jade, Mr. Summer, even our school principal.

"But we checked in there twice!" someone shouted.

Jade scowled. "You are such a time vampire!"

"Huh?"

"You just sucked up a massive amount of everyone's time, including mine."

Of course, Harper had to put in his two cents. "You're gonna receive a life sentence . . . grounded until the end of time."

"For real!" Jade agreed.

Remembering the policeman's warning, I attempted to get their sympathy. "I could have been a statistic," I said as pathetically as I possibly could.

Jade must have known what that meant, because she patted me gently on the shoulder and I saw a glimmer of niceness in her eyes, something I hadn't seen in a really long time.

Seeing Jade turn nice to me made Harper get that question mark look in his eyes. "What's that mean . . . been a statistic?" he asked.

"Kidnapped . . . or dead," Jade replied. "Don't ever do that again!" she warned. "Grandpa had to take his heart pills."

For once, Harper wasn't smirking.

Over and over, I said sorry. Sorry to my parents, sorry to Nana and Grandpa, sorry to the school principal, and sorry to Mr. Summer.

Mr. Summer sighed loudly. "See you tomorrow, Zoe."

I frowned. Oh no. School—Zena—U-G-L-Y me. I didn't ever want to go to school again.

Mr. Summer must have seen the look on my face, because he informed me that because our school has zero tolerance for bullying and name-calling, Zena had received a one-day suspension, and that he had spoken to the rest of the class. "Don't worry, Zoe. There won't be any trouble."

I hoped he was right.

And probably thinking I couldn't hear her, Nana leaned in to Daddy and told him, "Don't be too hard on her, Darrow . . . She's a delicate girl."

Daddy looked at her for a minute as if she had told him something he didn't know. He glanced my way, then nodded in agreement.

Delicate—me?

In my room later that night, Daddy mostly listened while Mom nagged me—on and on and on until, like a car out of gas, she finally came to a stop.

Right before midnight I climbed into bed. "I promise I'll never do it again. I just didn't want anyone to see me cry. I'm really sorry."

"You're grounded for a month, Zoe," she said.

A month but not eternity. My sentence fit the crime.

Mom hugged me and Daddy kissed the top of my head. "G'night, Zoe . . . love you."

"Okay . . . sorry," I said one last time.

Mom left, but Daddy Reindeer lingered in my doorway. "G'night, *my* Zoe," he whispered.

My Zoe? He'd never called me that before. I liked it. Must be connected to being delicate, I thought.

"Daddy, what does *delicate* mean?"

He stared up at the ceiling, took a deep breath, and replied, "Something that you shouldn't be too rough with because it might get damaged. Like a flower that needs to be protected from the sun or cold weather . . . so it can grow and bloom."

"Oh. Am I like that?" I asked.

"Yes, *my Zoe*. I love you. G'night."

"G'night."

And then the light was out, the door was closed, and Daddy Reindeer was gone.

I wanted to holler, Come back! Come back so I can ask you another question.

Am I ugly?

20

The Day After Trouble Day

The next morning at school, everyone, including me, tried very hard to act normal, as if nothing strange had happened. Of course, I got a few funny looks, but no one said anything mean. Plus, Zena had been suspended for the day.

Lucky Zoe.

But that day at lunch in the cafeteria, something puzzling happened. A new kid named Adam York, who is in Mr. Summer's class too, came over and sat down across from me, Zoe G. Reindeer.

The only person I've ever sat with during lunch is Quincy—almost always at this same small table in the corner. And since Quincy's been gone, the only person I sit with is me.

He smiled, said, "Hi," and started chomping a burger.

"Hi."

As always, the cafeteria was crazy noisy, most people yapping, some people hollering, wild loud laughter, the sounds of dishes and trays. But sitting there next to Adam felt quiet—quiet like when the class is taking a really hard test and every mind is busy thinking. Quiet like when you're so nervous, everything seems to have come to a stop—including your heart.

For some reason, I began checking the buttons on my sweater to make sure they were buttoned right. My clothes kind of matched today; that was good. I wondered why I'd never really noticed him before. But then again, to me, most kids at school were like streetlights— always there but hardly ever noticed.

Why did he come and sit beside me? Why am I feeling weird inside? More and more whys kept coming, but no answers followed. My shyness was orbiting around me like a giant moon. I couldn't speak. Then, all of a sudden, I remembered something about him. He has a sister named Eve. Like Adam and Eve, I thought, in the Garden of Eden.

From her spectacular tree house in the Garden of Eden, Zoe could see clear to the horizon, where the blue sky meets the bluer ocean. African elephants, gazelles, and zebras roamed the plains. Zoe didn't need a radio because all day long the birds were singing songs. A monkey waved and handed her a banana . . .

"What's BQ mean?" Adam blurted, interrupting my fantasy.

So that was it. He was a spy on a mission—sent, in all likelihood, by Zena or her puppets. I glanced over to the table where they were sitting and waited for one of them to look our way, but their eyes stayed focused on each other.

Hmmm. Maybe he's not a spy.

"It means 'be quiet,'" I replied.

"Oh."

And Adam went on eating his lunch and I went on eating mine and then he was finished and he got up to leave, but before he did, he told me, "You're not ugly, Zoe."

"Okay."

As he walked away, I watched him to see if he was going to stop at the table where Zena's clique was sitting, to tell them what BQ meant so they could make fun of me again—but he didn't.

He seems nice—maybe.

❧

Before bed that night, I stared hard at myself in the bathroom mirror from the front and sort of from the sides, which is kind of hard.

Not ugly?

Does *not ugly* equal *pretty*?

I dabbed some of Jade's pink lip gloss on my lips. It tastes like bubble gum, I thought as I slipped the tube in my pocket. It was just borrowing. I'd bring it back tomorrow. Jade had so much makeup, she wouldn't miss one tube for one day, would she?

Then I used her flat iron on my hair. Was straight better than not straight, or did it just look different? Just different, I decided.

When I was finished, I opened the bathroom door to find the snox waiting outside. How does he always know when I'm up to something? How? I wondered.

Harper glanced at the flat iron and smirked. "What'd you do to your hair, Zoe?" he asked. "It looks way different." Then he stared at my shiny lips. "Are you wearing makeup?"

"BQ, Harper. Just BQ."

21

Nana's Cure

$\mathcal{B}$ecause I'd run away from school and because I'd been what everyone was calling *blue*—which means "mostly not happy"—since my best friend had gone, I'd been summoned to Nana and Grandpa Reindeer's apartment for the weekend.

"I want you to stop this moping around, Zoe," Nana told me. "It does not become you. It's not like you've had your heart broken . . . yet. Just like those tears we talked about that Jade used to make you spill, better to save that moping for later, when you'll need it." Nana got in my face and grinned. "Now give me a smile."

I almost smiled.

"I'd tell you a good joke if I knew one, but I was never good in the joke department. Don't suppose you know one?"

I shook my head and kept peeling potatoes.

Nana inched closer to me until we were standing side by side. "Seems to me you've grown a little, *my* Zoe."

Why were people suddenly calling me *my* Zoe like they owned me?

The store was called Zoe's. Inside, there were rows and rows of life-size dolls for sale and all of them looked just alike, just like Zoe G. Reindeer—except they each had on a different extremely cute outfit. They were selling for $199.99.

"Zoe?" Nana said.

"Yes?"

"I said, seems to me you've grown a little."

"A little," I replied.

I watched my nana as she washed the celery and onions for the potato salad we were making. Her silver hair was pulled back into a bun and red earrings dangled from her ears.

"You like eggs in your potato salad, don't you?" she asked as she opened a carton of eggs.

"Yes."

Earlier, we'd gone shopping and Nana had bought me two new dresses and a pair of sparkly lavender sneakers. Even though she always treats me nice, today felt special because I barely ever have her all to myself. Nana had held my hand now and then as we shopped, and I almost told her I'm too old for hand-holding, but I didn't. I really liked not sharing her.

"Every so often, a young lady needs to be doted on," she'd told me later as we sat side by side, eating burgers and fries at a fifties diner.

"What's *doted on*?" I'd asked.

"Spoiled rotten."

I'd finally smiled.

"Now, that's *my* Zoe." I'd leaned my head into her shoulder, soaking up her flowery smell. "No more running off from school, promise me? We were worried sick," she'd whispered.

For the zillionth time, I swore I would never do it again.

"Can I use your computer to check my e-mail?" I asked after I'd peeled the last potato.

"Of course," Nana replied. "Expecting a note from Quincy, I suppose?"

"Hope so."

"Must be really hard on Quincy with his mom being sick and having to move and go to a new school," Nana commented.

I nodded in agreement and thought about what she'd said for a little while. Nana's right. It must be really hard for him.

When I turned on the computer and entered my e-mail address and password and saw that there was a new message from Quincy—that made me grin. But when I read it, the inside part of me finally started dancing again. I leaped up and ran into the kitchen.

"He's coming back . . . next week!" I shouted.

Nana patted the top of my head.

"And his mom is almost done with her treatments," I told her. "I know he'll be happy to see her."

Nana winked. "And you."

For some reason, her saying that made me feel a little ashamed. With Kendra being so sick, I shouldn't even be thinking about myself, but I couldn't help it. I missed him so much and couldn't wait to have my only friend back.

As if Nana were reading my mind, she asked, "I never hear you talk about any other friends. You must have some, don't you?"

I shrugged. "I'm not very good at friends."

"Maybe you could join a club."

"Not good at clubs either. Mostly, people think I'm odd."

"Sounds like me at your age. I had a hard time fitting in too."

I stared into Nana's brown eyes. "Did you wear glasses?" I asked.

"No, but I was always tall for my age, and kids teased me something awful," she replied.

"How tall are you now?"

"Five foot ten," she answered.

I remembered Mrs. Warner's comment about big feet and being tall and snuck a peek at my nana's feet. "Were your feet really big too?"

Nana laughed. "So big, I used to trip over them. But my being tall paid off later."

"How?"

"Made a little book money modeling during college, and it probably helped me nab your grandpa," Nana answered.

"How?" I repeated.

"He was six foot four. Liked me being tall." She paused, then added, "Some things are in the genes. Can't change that, Zoe."

"Were you shy too?"

"Still am sometimes. No crime in that." Nana patted the top of my head. "Lots of people feel a little odd at your age. Like those shoes you keep growing out of, you'll grow out of feeling so different. I sure did."

Nana had a way of being right about lots of things. I hoped this was one of them.

22

A Sign

$\mathcal{T}$hat night, as soon as Grandpa Reindeer dropped me off, the first thing I did was make a beeline to the greenhouse to give the baobabs a dose of water. They'd sprout soon, I hoped.

When I finished, I headed to the house. "Quincy's coming home on Saturday!" I loudly proclaimed as I burst through the kitchen door. But the kitchen was empty, the dinner table had been cleared, and the dishwasher was running. I followed the blare of the flatscreen into the family room, where Jade and Harper sat, their eyes glued to the TV. When I came into the room, they didn't even look up. Shopping bags filled with the stuff Nana had bought me dangled from my arms.

To get their attention, I stood in front of the screen and grinned.

"What're you so happy about?" Harper asked.

Jade eyed the bags. "What! Did Nana buy you a bunch of stuff?"

I nodded.

"So that's all it took to make you happy again?" the snox asked.

"Plus Quincy's coming home on Saturday for the weekend."

"Yay," Jade said. "Now can you move out of the way before you make us miss the best part?"

"Yeah," Harper agreed.

I had been gone for two whole days and I thought Jade and the snox might have missed me a little, but obviously they hadn't. Silly Zoe.

"Where are Mom and Daddy?" At least they'd be glad to see me, right?

"In their room," Jade said.

"Fighting," Harper added.

"About what?" I asked.

Jade glanced up. "Money, what else?"

Not again.

I hurried down the hallway to my parents' room. Their door was closed, but I could hear them.

"It's time to stop dreaming, Darrow!" Mom shouted angrily.

"I'm not dreaming!" Daddy yelled back.

"It's a very good offer! The best ever! We could pay off all of the bills and buy a real house!"

"A real house? What's that supposed to mean?"

"It means this one needs a new roof, needs painting, the plumbing is a mess, the kitchen is an embarrassment . . . Do I have to go on? Sometimes it seems like you care more about those trees and plants than you care about us. We're one step away from foreclosure, Darrow! We could lose everything!"

"You worry too much, Gabby! I'll sell some of the mature exotic trees to that landscape architect who's been needling me. Maybe I'll get a night job! And if it turns out that we have to sell, I've got my eyes on a couple of things . . . another tropical plant nursery, or maybe this time a flower farm. Saw some for sale in Oregon, one in Carlsbad, another in Hawaii, and even one in New Zealand. Always wanted to go to New Zealand."

Sell the Wonderland? Weeks ago, he said he'd never sell the Wonderland. New Zealand?

Mom had the same thought. "New Zealand? I give up," she said in a quieter voice.

"It'd be an adventure. Life's supposed to be an adventure, Gabby!"

I'd never heard him say that before.

But Mom didn't agree. "I don't want an adventure! I just want a normal life and not to worry about money. You're not going to get a better offer than the one Bob Lockwood gave you today. We'd be on easy street. I don't understand what you're waiting on . . . for us to lose everything?"

There was about a minute of quiet before Daddy said in a soft voice, "I'm waiting on a *sign*, Gabby."

"You and your *signs*."

What does that mean, I wondered—waiting on a *sign*?

I lingered outside their room, motionless, until the hallway grandfather clock ticking beside me and the noise from the TV in the other room were the only sounds. I kept thinking that this is exactly what Quincy said his parents were like before they got divorced.

Right then, I wished that I hadn't heard their fight. My worry list kept growing.

Silently, I counted down from twenty to zero. Then, I knocked.

"It's me. *Just* Zoe. I'm back."

"Come in," Daddy said.

I turned the knob, cracked the door, and stuck my

head inside. They both tried hard to put those happy-to-see-you looks on their faces, but Mom looked tired and Daddy's eyes had zero happiness.

"Did you have a good time with Grandpa and Nana?" Mom inquired.

I stepped inside their room. "Yes," I replied. The smile I'd come home with had vanished.

Daddy stood from the chair where he was sitting. "Then why the sad look?"

I stared at the Reindeer parents and asked three questions. "Are you going to get a divorce . . . what's foreclosure . . . and what's a *sign*?"

23

The Trouble/Worry/Problem Zapper

*H*ow long have you been listening?" Daddy inquired. His oh-no look was pasted on his face.

"Long enough." I set the shopping bags on the floor.

Mom faked a smile. "Looks like your nana splurged on you."

Does she really think it's going to be that easy to change the subject? Think again, please.

"So, are you guys getting a divorce?" I repeated.

"No!" they replied in unison.

"What gave you that idea?" Daddy asked.

"I'm worried because you're acting just like Quincy's mom and dad did before they went splitsville."

"Splitsville?" Mom asked.

"Yeah, his mom and dad went splitsville because

they were always fighting about money, and now you guys are doing the same thing."

Daddy laughed.

Three Things Adults Should Never Do
When Kids Are Being Extremely Serious

1. Laugh.
2. Try to change the subject.
3. Tell you to relax.

My parents were now guilty of two of the three offenses. I glared at him. "It's not funny, Daddy."

Daddy apologized. "Sorry, Zoe. But we are definitely not getting a divorce."

I stared at him and asked, "Promise?"

He patted my shoulder, then gave it a gentle squeeze. "I promise, Zoe. No divorce. Relax."

Relax? Now they were guilty of all three offenses.

But somehow, the look in his eyes had convinced me he was telling the truth. Going splitsville was off the Zoe worry list. My interrogation of the Reindeer parents continued anyway. "What's *foreclosure* mean?"

This time, Mom did the denying. "It means you're late on the mortgage payment and the bank could take the house. But we are not in foreclosure yet."

All I heard was *yet*.

I had one last question for Daddy. "What did you mean by 'waiting for a sign'?"

Daddy gazed into my eyes. "Some clue that'll tell you what to do. Something that'll happen that leads you in the right direction. Like a sudden answer to a mystery . . . understand?"

I didn't but I nodded.

"One other thing . . . I really don't want to leave the Wonderland, and I sure don't want to move to New Zealand. Do they even speak English there?"

"Yes, they do." Then Mom sighed. "So you heard everything?"

"Pretty much."

Daddy picked nervously at his nails. "Don't say anything to Harper or Jade; we don't need them worrying too."

"I promise." I was just about to leave when I remembered. "Quincy's coming for the weekend," I blurted.

Daddy cracked a real smile, and Mom hugged me and said that was good news. "G'night," we all seemed to say at the same time.

Down the hallway in the family room I heard Jade and Harper laughing at something on the TV. They certainly weren't worrying about anything.

But even though my questions had sort of been answered, I still couldn't stop worrying. Where would we live if the bank took the Wonderland? And I still didn't understand what *waiting on a sign* meant.

Why did there have to be so many problems and troubles and worries?

Zoe was a super-geek tech-genius—the creator of the TROUBLE/WORRY/PROBLEM ZAPPER *app—an app that could be downloaded to your phone that allowed anyone to type in their problem, press delete, and presto-change-o—problem gone. The only thing it couldn't delete was annoying people, because deleting people, no matter how annoying they are, is a crime. Almost everyone on Earth had downloaded the app, making Zoe G. Reindeer a gazillionaire. Her three-story house in the Malibu Hills had a panoramic view of the ocean.*

Tonight, no lights from Mrs. Warner's candles next door danced on my walls and none of her old-time jazz music played. The Moon was having one of its days off, so there was total darkness, and the only sounds were the noises inside my mind that even *Imaginary Zoe* couldn't make go away.

24

A New Friend

As I headed to my table in the cafeteria, I heard Zena warn her puppets, "You know she'll rat you out if you say anything to her, so don't."

Was Zena right? Was I going to be a rat every time someone bullied me? Would I run to Mr. Summer, the way he'd instructed me to, and squeal?

When I'd told Quincy what had happened, he'd said, "Sometimes you have to be a rat, Zoe."

What did I have to lose by being a rat, anyway? Quincy was my only friend.

Except maybe not. Adam was wearing a green-and-blue plaid shirt when he sat down at lunch across from me again.

"You live in that Wonderland plant place, huh?" he asked.

"Yeah."

"Must be interesting," Adam said.

I decided to try very hard not to be shy. I took a deep breath. "Sometimes," I answered, then spouted off nervously. "There's all sorts of stuff, even endangered plants. My dad's a horticulturist. Which is a fancy way to say he knows a lot about plants and trees and flowers." I wondered if he was going to keep asking questions, but when he didn't, I asked one of mine. "Where'd you go to school last year?"

"In Rome," he replied.

"Italy?"

Adam nodded.

"Were you born there?"

"No, I was born in Rhode Island, but because of my dad's work, we usually move every two years. So far, we've lived in Sweden; Japan; Washington, DC; Rome . . . and now here. My sister claims we're like animals that migrate, except we don't ever come back to the same place . . . at least not yet. My mom calls us nomads."

I was sitting across from a worldwide voyager, and instantly I felt like a very boring girl with a life story so dull, it would make you yawn a thousand times—the farthest I'd ever been from Pasadena was the Grand Canyon.

"Oh," I said.

"My mom and sister hate moving so much, but I like it because every place is a new adventure. My favorite so far is Japan. It was the coolest."

Adventure? Recently, lots of people were using that word—first Ben Rakotomalala, then Daddy, and now Adam.

"Can you speak Japanese?" I asked.

"A little, but after a while you start to forget. Good thing I have lots of pictures of all the places I've been to. I could show you, if you wanna see."

"Okay. Or you could e-mail some of them to me too," I told him.

"Cool."

I scribbled my e-mail address on some notebook paper and handed it to him.

"Want mine?" he asked.

"Sure."

Questions buzzed around me like flies at a picnic. Is he just being nice? Will he really e-mail me pictures? Does this mean I actually have a new friend? I hoped I'd have the answers I wanted soon.

25

Inside Mrs. Warner's House

The star of day was hard at work heating everything up, so I walked home on streets that had shady trees. Instead of being green the way they usually are in the fall, the foothills ahead of me were dry and brown from not having enough rain. By the time I turned the corner to the Wonderland, I was sweating and thirsty.

Mrs. Warner wasn't outside when I passed her house, but her front door was wide open and smoke was coming out. I ran to her door.

"Mrs. Warner!" I yelled. "You in there?" No reply. "Mrs. Warner!"

"Didn't your parents teach you not to scream?"

I whipped around. Mrs. Warner was standing behind

me. She must have been in her backyard. I pointed inside her house. "There's smoke!"

Mrs. Warner's eyes got wide with fright. "Help me get the hose!"

"We should call the fire department," I told her.

Mrs. Warner ignored me. She yanked her green hose and toddled inside.

"Mrs. Warner! Come back!"

But she didn't listen. "Turn on the water!" she hollered.

I dropped my backpack, turned on the water, and was about to zoom home to tell my daddy when Mrs. Warner reappeared, coughing.

"It's out. Just a little nothing. One of my candles must have tipped over. You can turn off the hose."

"We should still call the fire department," I said, "just in case."

"It's out, I told you! I do not need the fire department nosing around in my business."

"Okay, then I'll go get my daddy."

"And I don't need your daddy either. You want to do something to be of use . . . come inside and help me clean up the mess," she demanded.

Finally, a chance to go inside Mrs. Warner's house.

What if the fire isn't really out? I worried. Never go inside a burning house, Daddy always said. His warning screamed in my ears. But I peeked inside and could see the spot in the living room where the small fire had been. The floor and everything around it was water-soaked. Smoke hovered like fog.

"Help me open the windows!" Mrs. Warner commanded.

I stepped inside.

She unlocked a window and lifted it open. "Lucky for me you passed by when you did. You're an angel. I think that'll be my name for you from now on . . . Zoe Angel."

Zoe Angel? That sounded awesome. Much better than Zoe Reindeer.

I helped Mrs. Warner open window after window, and by the time we were finished, the smoke had been sucked outside. We picked up the burned, soaked stuff, mostly papers, and carted it out to the trash.

Once we were back indoors and I was able to take a good look around, I thought, Daddy was right—there was way too much stuff piled around: old newspapers, magazines, junk mail. Like going through a maze, I made my way from the living room to the kitchen, where maps and old calendars plastered the walls. Ceramic creatures and stuffed animals, mostly teddy bears, were perched here and there, but the kitchen itself was what Mom calls "spotlessly clean."

Shelves filled with books lined both sides of the hallway, making it a very narrow passageway.

"Have you read all of these books?"

"Some of them twice," Mrs. Warner replied. "Nothing better than a book and a little music that takes you back to happier times."

In the bedroom, lit candles inside colored glass containers still flickered, and beside them an old record player sat. A shelf was filled with vinyl records that nearly reached the ceiling.

"Maybe you should blow out all the candles," I warned her.

"Nonsense!" Mrs. Warner barked. "And not a word of this to a soul. They'll put me in the old-people orphanage for certain. I don't ever want to leave my house. Promise me you won't say a word, little angel."

"Don't you have any children you could go live with?" I asked.

Mrs. Warner plopped down on the bed.

"Had a daughter, but she died when she was about your age," she replied.

"What happened?"

"Tornado. Back in Missouri, where we lived. Took her and her daddy just like in that movie *The Wizard of Oz.* Some things are hard to watch. Some things never leave your mind . . . no matter how hard you try to force them away from your memory." Mrs. Warner lifted a framed picture from her nightstand and patted the bed. "Sit down."

I sat down beside her, and together, we looked at the photograph.

"This is her. Name was Lily. My girl was real pretty, don't you think? Pretty like you." Mrs. Warner smiled.

Pretty? Me?

Mrs. Warner slipped her arm around me and hugged me to her side. Then she glanced at the glimmering candles and said, "She would always light candles at dinnertime, my Lily, even in the summer. Promise me—not a word to a soul about this. I will be careful. In all my years . . . never had a fire before. Promise me, Zoe Angel," she repeated.

I knew I shouldn't make the promise, but I felt very sorry for Mrs. Warner. I didn't want her to have to go to the old-people orphanage.

"I promise."

❧

Since the *thing* with the police, Jade and Harper hadn't been like bee stings most of the time, and when they did start up, one glance from Daddy or Mom was all it took. And because of that, dinnertime had become slightly less gruesome.

At the table that night, Jade blabbed on and on about herself, sucking up five hundred percent of the attention, loving every minute all eyes were on her. I studied her like she was a bug under a microscope.

How many times, over and over and over, had I wished I were a Jade look-alike? But tonight, for the first time ever, probably because Adam had called me not-ugly and today Mrs. Warner had called me pretty, I stared at my sister without feeling that way. Jade looks like Jade and I—big feet, unruly hair, and all—look like me.

Jade seemed to have finished talking and I was about to, without mentioning the fire, tell them about going inside Mrs. Warner's house and Lily and the tornado, but Harper took over and started jabbering about science stuff. Like old leggings, dinner got stretched out. After a while, I didn't hear them anymore.

Instead, I pictured Lily's old, stained photo and imagined Lily and her daddy getting sucked up by the tornado. I gazed outside and wished Mrs. Warner could forget that extremely sad thing. Now I knew why she lit the candles. But at least she had the photograph—the photograph that made her smile.

"Zoe?" Mom said.

"Huh?"

"How was your day?" she asked.

"Fine," I replied. "Can we light candles at dinner sometimes?" I asked her.

Jade rolled her eyes.

Mom looked at me all twinkly-eyed. "We can. Maybe on Sundays. That'd be nice."

"That'd be real nice," Daddy echoed.

26

Grounded

$\mathcal{L}$ater that week, Adam was sitting across from me during lunch—Adam sitting across from me had somehow become an everyday event—and I was wearing the bubble-gum-tasting lip gloss that I'd sort of permanently borrowed from Jade. Day by day it was getting easier and easier to talk to him. Also, my shyness was seeming to show up less and less and less. I supposed having to talk to someone I barely knew every day was why.

Adam quizzed me about the carnivorous plants in the Wonderland and finally asked if he could see them, and I was about to say yes—until I remembered I was still grounded.

"I'm grounded," I told him.

"Because you ran away from school that day?"

"Yeah." Until right then, being grounded hadn't really mattered and I hadn't even thought about it. Now Adam wanted to come over, so it mattered. And then I remembered Quincy was coming back this weekend. That made being grounded the worst.

Maybe the Reindeer parents would let me make it up another time—like a make-up test. I sure hoped so!

৩

That night, I caught Daddy and Mom together on the sofa. Since their fight, I hadn't heard any more arguments about money. They were laughing at some TV show and they seemed happy.

Jade and Harper weren't around. Jade was out with her friends and Harper was in the garage, deep into his latest science project. So I'd caught the Reindeer parents alone and in good moods—perfect timing to plead my case.

I smiled my sweetest smile and spoke in my sweetest voice. "Since Quincy's coming home this weekend, can I be grounded another time?" I asked. "I'll even be grounded for another whole month," I pleaded. "Please say yes. Plus, Kendra is finally getting out of the hospital, and I really want to see her. I'm begging."

"So you're willing to extend your sentence for another whole month?" Daddy asked.

"Sentence? It's not jail, is it? I'll even clean the greenhouse for free."

They stared at each other hard, like they were using their Reindeer parent superpowers to communicate. Finally, Daddy said, "It's a deal. Just clean the greenhouse for free and you're off punishment, but only while Quincy is here, understand?" He had his best Daddy-is-being-serious look on his face. "Understand?" he repeated.

"Yes," I replied. "Thank you so much!"

And I knew I shouldn't push it any further, but I did. "Also, there's a boy from school who wants to come over and look at the carnivorous plants. So I was wondering—"

Mom interrupted, "Not part of the deal, Zoe." She waved her index finger no. "Not part of the deal."

"Thank you. I understand. G'night," I told them. But before I headed to my room, a thought suddenly popped into my mind. Wait a minute. "Clean the greenhouse for free for how long? Not forever, right?" I asked Daddy. Was one weekend with my best friend worth forever?

"How about two weeks," Daddy answered.

"Okay," I agreed. Quincy was definitely worth a whole lot more than thirty bucks. "G'night. And thank you again."

"G'night, Zoe."

I headed to my room, did some homework, and took out the book Ben Rakotomalala had given me. I was more than halfway done. I thought about him being an astronomer with a telescope, gazing at all sorts of stuff in the nighttime sky. Lately, at night, I'd been looking up more and more at the moon and stars, thinking about what was way up there past the Milky Way.

At that moment, I wondered how much a telescope costs. I'd look it up online tomorrow. Seeing as Daddy was worried about money, asking for one for Christmas seemed out of the question. As soon as I started getting paid for cleaning the greenhouse again, I'd start saving my money to buy one. Ben's book was getting me more and more curious about all kinds of things. I cracked it and read on.

Right then, someone turned the doorknob to my room and cracked the door. Harper stuck his face inside.

"You're supposed to knock!"

"Sorry." He closed the door and knocked.

"What!"

"Can I come in?" he asked.

"Why?"

"Just want to."

Huh? What was the snox up to now? My curiosity won. "Okay!"

"Hey, Zoe," he said. His eyes were fixed on the book Ben had given me.

So that was it. He'd probably been snooping in my room when I wasn't home and seen it.

"What's that book about?"

I held it up for him to read the title. "Just what it says, genius."

"Where'd you get it? I couldn't find it online."

Just like I thought—he had been snooping. "From this astronomer guy named Ben Rakotomalala who's from Madagascar but works at JPL," I bragged.

Harper squinted at me jealously. "The Jet Propulsion Lab? How'd you meet him?"

"He came into the nursery when I was working there." I decided to boast some more. "He says people with good imaginations, like me, are sometimes more important than people who have their heads full of facts."

"Is that what you're doing when you zone out . . . imagining stuff?" Harper asked.

I nodded.

"Oh. I thought you were just daydreaming."

"They're kind of the same thing," I told him.

"I suppose," Harper agreed, then asked, "What else did that man say?"

"He calls the sun 'the star of day.'"

"The star of day? Wow. Hugely cool." Harper glanced at the book. "Can I read it when you're done?" His eyes had that begging look.

An itty-bitty piece of me wanted to say yes, but most of me was still mad at him for stealing my science project idea and for being such a constantly annoying snox.

Zoe G. Reindeer thought for a minute. I finally had something Harper desperately wanted. But I wasn't about to give him something for nothing. "If you help me clean the greenhouse for a month, I'll let you read it."

Harper eyed the book. He hesitated for a few seconds, then said, "Deal."

"And one other thing . . . stop snooping in my room. Promise?"

"Promise."

He was at the door when he turned and smiled at me.

"What?" I asked.

"Thanks, Zoe."

"You're welcome."

"And the next time that man comes to the nursery, can you come get me so I can meet him too?"

Hmmm. I wasn't too sure about that. With Harper-geek-super-smart-boy around, Ben might lose all interest in me—even if I am an imaginer. And I really didn't need one more person treating me like *just* Zoe. "Maybe."

"Okay . . . G'night," Harper said in a nice way.

I watched him close the door to my room. "G'night."

27

Zoe and Quincy Together Again

$\mathcal{I}$, Zoe G. Reindeer, hate to get up really early on the weekends, but last night I set my alarm for 6:00 A.M. I didn't know what time Quincy would be back, but I wanted to be finished with my chores before he got here. Sleepiness made me press the snooze button, giving me ten more minutes of shut-eye, but finally, like a zombie, I crawled out of bed. Lazily, I put on my work clothes, ate some cereal, and woke up Harper.

He pulled the covers over his head. "It's too early," he whined.

"You made a deal," I reminded him.

He yawned and stretched. "I'm coming."

"You have fifteen minutes," I warned him.

Of course, birds were already chirping, talking non-stop to one another in bird chatter. One was singing a song.

BQ, happy birds.

Daddy was already up, with his head poked inside the hood of his truck, tinkering.

"Hi, Daddy."

"You're up early for a Saturday," he said.

"Quincy's coming today and Kendra too," I reminded him.

"That's right," he said, and went back to working on his truck.

"I'm going to the greenhouse."

"Before you go . . . do me a favor?"

"What?"

"Get in the truck and turn the key."

Me, inside the truck, turning the key? "Okay."

I turned the key but the truck didn't start; it only made a clicking sound.

"Thanks." Daddy kicked the truck. "This heap of junk!"

I got out and went to his side. "Whatsamatter with it?"

"Everything . . . starter, alternator, transmission, radiator, you name it. But it's got more than two hundred thousand miles on it, so I suppose I shouldn't be complaining."

I didn't know much about trucks or cars except when you turn the key they're supposed to turn on and they need to be fed gas and sometimes they need new tires. "Is two hundred thousand a lot?"

"Yes."

"Just take it to a shop and get it fixed," I advised him.

"Costs money, Zoe. Costs money."

"Oh." I grabbed a pen from the truck and did some math on the palm of my hand. There are fifty-two weeks in a year and I get paid fifteen dollars a week to take care of the greenhouse and do other chores around the Wonderland. That equals $780. I'd never realized it was that much money.

"You don't have to pay me for a whole year. That's seven hundred and eighty dollars."

At first Daddy smiled, then he started laughing so hard, he leaned against the truck and grabbed his belly.

"What's so funny?"

"Nothing, *my* Zoe."

He patted the top of my head and said, "It'll all work itself out. It just will. Now go on to the greenhouse and finish up so you can have your time with

Quincy. And catch a few flies for the flytraps and those others for me, okay?"

"Okay." I'd save that job for Harper.

The first thing I did was check on the baobabs—still nothing. What the heck was wrong? There was nothing for us to start the movie with. I frowned.

Soon, Harper joined me in the greenhouse. Together we worked and before long we were mostly finished. "Can I please go back to sleep now?" Harper pleaded.

"Sure." Being the boss really felt good. As Harper trudged outside, I called out to him, "Thanks, little brother."

I'd just finished watering the seedlings and was studying an orchid bud that was about to bloom when, behind me, the greenhouse door opened.

"Hey, Comet."

I couldn't believe my ears.

I turned around.

He was standing in the doorway, same round face and nerd glasses, smiling. Quincy.

I felt like someone was tickling me from the inside. Silly-happy.

I didn't mean to. I really didn't. But I was so happy that I couldn't stop myself. I dropped everything, ran to where he was standing, and hugged him tight. Tight like I'd fallen from a boat into the middle of the ocean and someone had thrown me one of those round life-savers and to keep from drowning I had to squeeze the thing until I almost squished it—that tight.

He made a fake choking sound. "Can't breathe, Zoe."

I laughed, let go, and stepped back. "Sorry."

"I wanna see the baobabs," he said. I pointed to where they were planted and stood behind him as he examined can after can. "They didn't grow yet?" he asked.

"Nope," I answered. "Something must be wrong. They should have sprouted a long time ago."

"Have you been watering them?"

"Yes."

He poked his finger into the dirt. "Did you soak the seeds for twenty-four hours before you planted them?"

"No . . . I just planted them."

"Zoe! The directions said to soak them in hot water for twenty-four hours and then use a nail file or knife to remove part of the seed's outer shell before you plant them. Otherwise, it takes months for them to grow."

"I didn't know I had to do all that stuff."

Quincy poked my shoulder. "That's what directions are for, Zoe. Always read directions."

"We can always buy some more," I told him.

"No, that's okay," he replied.

"Sorry you have to wait to start your movie."

He shrugged and said, "No problem," as if he didn't even care.

He's probably got too much other stuff to think about, I figured. Stuff like his mom. "I double swear I will look at them every day, and as soon as they grow, I'll let you know. . . all right?"

"Okay," he replied, then glanced at his watch. "C'mon, let's go. My dad's waiting for us in the car so we can go pick up my mom," he told me.

"But I have to finish my work," I told him.

"Your dad said it's okay. My pops already talked to him. C'mon."

I hadn't worn gloves, so my hands were grimy, and my blue jeans were filthy, and my work hoodie had holes at the elbows. No way was I going anywhere dressed like this. "I have to change my clothes. It won't take long. I promise."

Quincy checked his watch again and said, "Better hurry, Blitzen."

It felt so good to have him near that I actually liked being called reindeer names.

"Did you know *Blitzen* comes from a word that actually means 'lightning'?" Quincy asked as he followed me outside.

"Of course not, dork-boy." I snickered.

He shook his head. "Did you just call me 'dork-boy'? Is that what you've been learning in school, Zoe?"

"No, I made it up just now."

He shook his head again, but he was smiling. In fact, he seemed happier than ever. "Hurry up and change. I'll go tell my pops." Quincy zoomed off in one direction and I rushed to the house.

Two Things I Felt Like Doing Right Then

1. Twirling happily in a hundred circles with my arms stretched out.
2. Whistling a tune if I could—but no matter how hard I keep trying, I just can't.

As quickly as possible, I put on clean clothes and fixed my braids. I was about to put on lip gloss but thought Quincy might think it was weird.

Nope, no lip gloss for me today.

"Zoeeee," Quincy's dad, Wes, squealed as I climbed in the backseat.

As we drove, music from the radio played and, as usual, Quincy's dad sang along. His voice was pretty bad, but I didn't care. Being with them again reminded me of the summer when I went with Quincy and his dad to the beach at Paradise Cove and we ate burgers in the restaurant there and walked along the beach until it got cold. It almost felt like no time had passed since then—like the summer had never ended.

∽

The only thing that was different about Kendra, other than her head still being bald, was that she had lost some weight.

After she hugged and kissed Quincy for a very long time, she turned to me.

"Your turn, Miss Zoe. Gimme a hug, girl." She took me in her arms and I realized she was missing her usual perfumy smell too.

"All finished with my treatments. Docs are saying it's looking good."

Quincy took his mom's hand and together we walked down the corridor toward the exit doors. On the way, nurses and other people called out to Kendra, wishing her well. Giving her smiles and hugs.

"Gonna miss you round here," one nurse told her.

"Gonna miss you too, but hope never to be back here except to visit, if you catch my meaning."

Before we reached the door, Wes took Kendra's hand and Kendra leaned into him.

Are they un-splitsville? I wondered.

Wes and Kendra also acted like they were married again when we stopped at the hardware store.

"Your parents are sure being nice to each other," I commented to Quincy as we trailed behind Kendra and Wes's shopping cart.

He grinned. "Yeah, I know. It's kinda awesome."

Wes stopped the cart and loaded on a bunch of moving boxes.

"I hate packing. And I mean hate it!" Kendra proclaimed.

"Who's moving?" I asked.

"Didn't Quincy tell you?" Wes asked.

"Tell me what?"

"I'm selling the house here and moving to San Francisco," Kendra answered.

My eyes flew to Quincy. "Huh?"

"I was about to tell you," he said. "My mom is going to move in with us because she can work from home anywhere but my dad can't leave his job."

"You're going to be in San Francisco forever?"

"Looks that way," Kendra told me.

Instantly I went blank inside—like a book with all of its words suddenly erased. I was on the verge of tears.

"Sorry. But I wanted to tell you in person because I was afraid you'd get all sad and stuff."

"That's why you didn't get mad about the bao-babs, huh? Because there isn't going to be any movie, right?"

"Sorry," he repeated. "But it's good news that my family will all be back together again. Plus it's not that far away, Zoe."

"And you can come visit anytime," Kendra added.

Wes patted my shoulder and smiled. "Plane ride only takes an hour, Zoe."

I'm not sure why, but right then this thought showed up from out of nowhere, which I suppose is where thoughts hide. I thought about Adam and all the places he'd been to and how I'd felt like a very boring girl the other day when he'd talked about his adventures—as he called them.

"It's not that far away," I said out loud as if I were trying to convince myself.

Suddenly, I didn't feel like a book with no words. Instead, I felt all mixed up, like when you fill your cup with five different kinds of soda. Most of me still wanted Quincy to live right down the street, but some of me was glad he had his parents back together again. Some of me was sad. But some of me was excited to think about taking a plane to visit Quincy. I'd never been on a plane.

Zoe, wearing safari clothes, boarded the jet. The flight attendant fluffed Zoe's pillow and offered her hors d'oeuvres—shrimp wrapped with bacon—Zoe's favorite. The pilot started the engine and in no time the plane was on its way to the African Serengeti. The baobabs would be beautiful this time of year, and perhaps after that she would head to Madagascar . . .

"Zoe?" Quincy whispered,

"I was just wondering . . . how much do plane tickets to San Francisco cost?" I asked Kendra.

"Not that much," she replied. "I'll see if you can use my frequent flier miles."

"And I can visit anytime?"

"Anytime," she replied.

I turned my watery eyes to my best friend. "And you guys could come here and visit too, right?"

"Right," Wes replied.

"Plus it's not that far away," Quincy repeated.

I wanted to—but I didn't cry.

That night, I lay awake, staring at the ceiling, thinking. Quincy and Kendra going to live with Wes was pretty hard for Zoe G. Reindeer but probably best for Quincy. He seemed so happy and so did Wes and Kendra. I supposed that sometimes what's best for someone you care about might at first seem like it's the worst thing in the world for you. But if you really stop and think about it—if you really care about that person—the most important thing is for them to be happy, and them being happy makes you happy. It's like some kind of circle. Plus it would be a real adventure, not just an imaginary one.

⤬

By the next evening, Quincy and his dad were on the road back to San Francisco. Kendra was staying behind for a few days with her sister to pack up the house, and I'd promised to help. Every day after school, instead of going straight home, I went to Kendra's. Some days my mom, dragging Jade along, came to lend a hand. By the end of the week, everything was packed and ready to go.

And all week long, I didn't cry. I just kept saving my tears.

Saturday morning, the moving van was parked in front of used-to-be-Quincy's house, and in no time, everything was loaded.

Alongside the Reindeer parents I stood on the sidewalk. My mom had her arm curled around my shoulder. During the past week, Mom had been incredibly nice to me. Nicer than ever. Before bedtime, we'd started reading books together again, and twice, my mom had even brought me hot chocolate with whipped cream and tiny marshmallows. When we were watching TV, instead of snuggling with Daddy, Mom curled up next to me. My daddy had even let me trim one of the bonsai trees, and this time, when I made a small mistake, he didn't have a fit. I supposed my mom and daddy felt sorry for me.

"Gimme a hug, girl," Kendra said before she climbed in her sister's car. They were driving to San Francisco together.

I reached for her and clung to her tightly—almost as tightly as I'd hugged Quincy in the greenhouse the other day. My mom and daddy hugged her too.

Kendra sighed and climbed in the car. "See you real soon, Zoe," she said through the open window.

"Bye, Kendra," I told her.

Kendra winked. "This is not a good-bye, Zoe."

Everyone waved and then she was gone.

The Reindeer parents seemed as sad as I was.

"I can visit anytime," I reminded them, "and it's not that far away."

Finally, there must not have been any more room for my saved-up tears, because they rolled down my cheeks.

Mom took out a tissue and dried them.

And together we strode home.
In the middle of the night, I woke up.

Zoe G. Reindeer's eyes were powerfully telescopic. They could see for hundreds and thousands of miles. Her eyes zeroed in on San Francisco and focused. The window to Quincy's room was open. There he was, curled up in his bed. Kendra would be there soon. Zoe zoomed in for a closer look and thought she saw Quincy smile.

28

The Boy Comes to the Wonderland

Two Good Things That Happened
Because Quincy Moved Away

1. I instantly wasn't grounded anymore.
2. Adam got to come to the Wonderland.

Which started me believing Nana's claim that sometimes good stuff can come from bad or sad things.

"Hi there, Zoe Angel," Mrs. Warner said as Adam and I walked past her house on the way to mine. She was holding a gnome statue in her arms like it was a baby. She didn't have her false teeth in, but she was smiling just the same, showing nothing but her pink gums.

Every time she sees me since that day when she told me about the tornado, Mrs. Warner has been calling me Zoe Angel, and because I like it, I've been letting her.

I smiled and waved. "Hi, Mrs. Warner."

"Why'd she call you Zoe Angel?" Adam asked.

I shrugged. "She thinks I'm nice."

"She's right," he said.

❧

"This place has all kinds of amazing stuff," Adam said when we arrived at the Wonderland.

The list of people who came to visit me at the Wonderland and thought it was cool that I lived in a place with so many trees that you could barely see our house had so far been a very short list—Quincy and one other kid named Sophie Wong, who'd moved away in the third grade. Now Adam's name was added to the list. A short list of three.

Zoe G. Reindeer was about to feel sorry for herself when she thought about people like Mrs. Warner, who had no list. No people who came to visit, not even one friend, maybe no one to love them.

Even a short list was better than no list at all, I decided. I smiled at Adam and led him to the pond.

Some orange butterflies fluttered around, and the

blue sky had a few fat fluffy clouds. Two wild ducks were in the pond.

"You have ducks?" he asked.

"No, they just come here every year about this time," I said, then had a thought. "Do you think they get bored?" I asked. "Coming back to the same place over and over?"

Adam stared at the ducks. "I think it's just animal instinct. Plus, when they're flying, it has to be different every time. Sometimes it's windy . . . sometimes it might rain. And once they land here after being away for a whole year, it probably looks different."

He was right. The Wonderland was always changing and stuff was always growing and sometimes stuff just sprouted up in strange places. Like people, everything that's alive is always changing inside or out or both, I decided.

I looked at Adam. Even I was changing. I had a new friend.

I had a question I'd been dying to ask since the first day he sat down beside me in the cafeteria, and now seemed like the perfect time. "How come your mom and dad named you guys Adam and Eve?"

Adam chuckled. "Everyone always asks that."

I opened the door to the greenhouse and we stepped inside. "So, what's the answer?"

"They said it was because my sister and I were their first creations."

"Oh, I get it."

Then it was his turn to ask a question he'd most likely wanted to ask me for a while. "Is it weird to have the last name Reindeer?"

I cocked my head to the side. "What do you think?"

"I think it'd be cool. Adam Reindeer."

Right then, he reminded me of Quincy, which started me wondering what he was doing right now. Even though I had a new friend, I still missed my old friend. After Adam left, I would send Quincy an e-mail, I promised myself. Maybe he'd be able to use his dad's cell phone and call me. I really wanted to hear his voice.

How many years have to pass before a new friend becomes an old one? I wondered.

"Amazing!" Adam said when he saw the flytraps. He peered, examining them closely, like they were the superstars of the greenhouse. "I read that they mostly catch their own insects, usually flies, and that they don't eat a lot during the winter."

"Yeah, they get dormant." I'd learned that from Daddy.

Adam and I were looking around at this and that when he spotted the old coffee cans where I'd planted the baobab seeds. He stuck his finger into the soil, which, because I'd just watered them yesterday, was wet. He drew his dirt-covered finger out and wiped it on his jeans. "What's planted in these?" he asked.

"Oh. I planted some baobab seeds, but they didn't grow yet."

"What's a baobab?" he asked.

"It's a tree from Madagascar. It's endangered."

"Endangered? Cool."

"My friend Quincy was planning to make a movie about them, but . . ." I sighed loudly.

"He migrated . . . I mean moved," Adam said, taking over where I'd left off.

Suddenly, from out of nowhere, like a magician who knows how to instantly appear or vanish, the snox showed up. He was wearing a straw cowboy hat that was so big for his head that it almost hid his eyes. "Hi, guys. Whatcha doing?"

"Just showing Adam the greenhouse."

"Hey," Adam said to Harper.

"Hey," Harper replied.

Since I'd been letting Harper read the book and he'd been helping me in the greenhouse, we'd kind of been getting along better, but I didn't want him to say or do anything annoying. I stared at Harper, thinking, Please don't say anything to embarrass me. BQ! BQ!

BQ! For once, I hoped that he could really read my mind.

Apparently he could, because Harper simply said, "See you later, guys," and headed out the door.

"Was that your brother?" Adam asked.

"Yeah," I replied, "that's *just Harper*."

After we left the greenhouse, we walked through the rows of plants and trees in the Wonderland, and when we wound up at the pond again, Adam caught a frog and held it in his palm. He laughed as he ran his hand along its bumpy skin. But when a hawk landed nearby in the birdbath, eyeing the frog like it was dinner, the frog leaped away and disappeared under the water lilies.

Adam smiled. "Amazing!"

And then the boy said it was time for him to leave and we headed toward the entrance to the Wonderland.

Daddy was standing near the nursery in the driveway, talking to a man I recognized as one of the land developers who'd been bugging Daddy to sell. Daddy stopped talking when he saw us and grinned. "Howdeedoo, Zoe."

"Hi, Daddy. This is Adam . . . my friend."

Daddy made a fist and stuck out his hand. "Howdeedoo, Adam. Call me Darrow."

Adam butted knuckles with Daddy. "Hey, Darrow."

The land developer's cell phone rang and he excused himself to take the call.

While Daddy Reindeer quietly examined Adam from head to toe, I nervously picked at my nails.

"Adam has to go now," I told Daddy.

"Maybe I'll see you again, Adam," Daddy told him.

"Yeah . . . maybe."

The man had finished his call and so stole my daddy's attention again. Adam and I slowly made our way to the front gate. "Bye, Adam."

He slung his backpack over his shoulder. "See you tomorrow, Zoe."

I watched him as he walked down the street. He turned around twice to look back at me. Once, Adam waved and I waved back.

"Seems like a nice young man," Daddy said to me at dinner that night between bites of macaroni and cheese.

"Who?" Jade demanded to know.

"Adam, Zoe's new friend," Harper answered.

Jade turned her attention to me. "So that's why you've been wearing lip gloss and matching your clothes."

I hadn't realized Jade had noticed.

My tongue felt like it was tied in a knot. "But . . . but . . . but—" I stuttered.

"But what? 'Bout time you ditched Quincy," Jade said, then added sarcastically, "but . . . oh yeah, I forgot, he wasn't your boyfriend."

"I'd never ditch Quincy. Plus, Adam's not my boyfriend either," I insisted. "He's just my friend."

Jade rolled her eyes. "Stop feeling guilty, little sister. There's nothing wrong with having more than one boyfriend. I have three. Well, four, if you count Aston James, but he's such a geek, I don't really count him unless I need his help with homework."

I shook my head. "He's not my boyfriend, I swear."

Jade clicked her tongue. "You are such a dork."

I scowled at her. "Am not."

Harper chimed in. "Are so."

"You two leave Zoe alone," Daddy demanded.

Harper opened his mouth to say something, but it looked like Mom nudged him under the table. He glared at her. "What? So you and Daddy are suddenly the Zoe protectors?"

"Enough!" Mom shouted.

After that, no one said a word. We finished eating and I helped Daddy with the dishes.

On the way to my room, I grabbed the portable

phone. Then I opened my laptop, plopped on my bed, and e-mailed Quincy to please call me. I waited and waited until it was after ten o'clock, but he didn't call. He didn't even e-mail me back. It was a school night, so maybe he was already asleep, or if he was really lucky, maybe he was out somewhere having fun with his mom and dad. Or maybe he had a new friend too.

I slipped into my pj's, slid under the down comforter, and continued reading the book Ben had given me. I was on the last chapter. Creative people and inventors really did change the world, plus they sometimes had fun doing stuff that somehow didn't always seem like work. I stopped reading. Their stories were beginning to make me want real adventures, not just my imaginary ones. I closed the book and turned out the light.

Tonight, the candles over at Mrs. Warner's house sent glimmers of light to my room. I stole a look at my digital clock. It's really getting late, but maybe he'll call, I hoped. Where is he? Maybe he's forgetting about me.

Zoe Angel used her wings to fly to San Francisco. Before long, she'd located her target, Quincy Hill. He was sitting in front of the television, watching a movie, of course, munching on popcorn. Zoe Angel made herself invisible, landed beside him, and whispered in his ear, "Call Zoe. She misses you."

I was cradling the phone when it rang.
It was Quincy. "Hey, Zoe."

Zoe Angel had the power.

29

The Baobabs—Still Nothing

J yawned and stretched. It was the first week of winter break.

Three Awesome Things About Winter Break

1. No school.
2. No school.
3. No school.

Tomorrow, Adam and his family were leaving for Paris (where his grandparents live) for Christmas. Lucky Adam.

And Quincy was coming to stay at our house for the whole week after Christmas.

Extremely lucky Zoe.

❧

Every day, Jade's friends had been in and out of the house from morning to night. I did my best to avoid them.

Harper spent most of his time in the garage, still working on his science projects. "My scholarship to MIT or Cal Tech is a done deal," he'd been bragging.

"Won't be long before Quincy is here," Daddy reminded me as I helped him out in the nursery.

"I know," I said, and thanked him for letting him come for a whole week.

The nursery door opened and four customers came in at once. Lately, business had been good. "Better than ever," I'd heard Daddy say. Every year at this time, people flocked to the Wonderland to buy our living Christmas trees and poinsettias and plants to give as gifts. And as usual, we got our share of people thinking we had real reindeer at the Wonderland. During Christmastime, Daddy wears a red-and-white Santa hat.

Fake lit-up reindeer lined the driveway. Twinkling Christmas lights were strung everywhere.

Money seemed to be pouring in. Daddy had sold some more of his exotic plants and trees to landscape architects and made enough to fix his truck. Mom and Daddy seemed happy again. No one was talking about selling the Wonderland or moving to any kind of flower farm in another state or especially to New Zealand.

"Merry Christmas," Daddy told the customers.

"Merry Christmas," they replied.

I'd been hoping that by now at least one of the baobabs might have sprouted. It was what I'd planned to give Daddy for Christmas. Online, I'd learned that they shouldn't be overwatered. I kept wishing I'd read the directions so they would have sprouted by now. Maybe I'd ruined them.

For a while, except for the Christmas music playing softly, the nursery was quiet. But then someone opened the door, sounding the chime. I peeked through the shelves. Ben Rakotomalala ducked inside.

I stopped everything and practically bolted toward him.

His big smile seemed even bigger. "Zoe! My friend!"

"Can I help you?" Daddy asked. He had a puzzled look.

I made the introduction. "This is Ben, Daddy."

"The man who gave you the book?"

"Yes."

"First book I've seen her read because she actually wanted to in a long, long time. Thank you, Mister . . . ?"

"Rakotomalala," I blurted.

"Ben will suffice," the tall man from Madagascar said.

Daddy stretched out his hand for Ben to shake. "Darrow . . . Darrow Reindeer."

They smiled and shook hands.

Ben placed a package wrapped in brown paper on the counter.

I eyed it. Looks like another book, I thought. I hope it's for me.

"Just stopped in to bring this Christmas gift for Zoe. I hope that's okay."

I ran my hand over the package. "It's another book, huh?"

"Yes. By Carl Sagan," Ben replied. "He has a rather famous quote that I love. 'We have lingered long enough on the shores of the cosmic ocean. We are ready at last to set sail for the stars.' I believe that to be true."

More and more these days, I discovered, I was feeling less and less shy—first with Adam and now with Ben.

"Thank you, Ben," I said.

"That's very kind of you," Daddy told him.

"Oh . . . before I forget . . . I also came by to check and see if you have that special item I've been waiting for," Ben added.

Oh no! It's supposed to be a surprise! BQ! Please!

"Special item?" Daddy asked.

"Yes—"

I nudged Ben with my elbow and looked sideways at my daddy. "It's a surprise . . . a Christmas surprise!" I pressed my finger to my lips.

From the look on both of their faces, I could tell they understood. Ben grinned and Daddy's eyes twinkled.

Whew! That was close. "We might have it after Christmas, if you want to come back," I said.

"After Christmas, then. I'll look forward to it."

Daddy extended his hand to Mr. Rakotomalala a second time. "Good meeting you, Ben." But this time they shook hands like friends.

"Happy holidays, Darrow and Zoe Reindeer!" Ben bellowed.

"Merry Christmas," Daddy and I replied happily.

The door chimed and the tall man from Madagascar ducked outside into the Wonderland.

I picked up my present. "Can I open it now? I already know it's a book. Please?"

Daddy nodded.

Quickly, I ripped off the paper. I held the book up for Daddy to see the title: *Cosmos*. "Cool . . . very cool," I said.

30

Zoe and Harper Discover

That night, I opened the new book Ben had given me and read what he had written on the first page again and again.

To My Friend Zoe Reindeer—May your life be an amazing adventure.

Ben Rakotomalala

I thumbed through it for a while, looking at the awesome photos, and I wondered if traveling to other places in the universe would one day be as easy as traveling to other continents is these days. Probably.

The knock on the door came as I knew it would.

Earlier, I'd told Harper about the new book, and I figured he'd come to see. "Who is it?" I asked as if I didn't know.

"Me . . . Harper."

"You can come in."

"I thought you were gonna come get me so I could meet him too, Zoe?" Harper complained.

"Sorry. He was only here for a few minutes, anyway."

"Oh. Can I see?"

I nodded, turned to the page where Ben had signed, and pointed. "Look."

To My Friend Zoe Reindeer—May your life be an amazing adventure.

Ben Rakotomalala

Suddenly, I had an idea. "Let's go outside," I told my brother.

"For what? It's dark."

"Exactly."

◦∾

We settled by the pond and stared upward.

"I don't know too much about the constellations of stars, but it's something I should study," Harper said in a matter-of-fact way, like it was just one more thing on his list of subjects to investigate further.

The Moon was nowhere—having another night off, I guessed. I wondered why the Earth only has one moon instead of two or more like some planets in the galaxy. If we had more than one, we might never have a moonless night.

I pictured moons of different colors lighting the nighttime.

Zoe was the Maker of Moons. If your planet needed more light at night, you simply hired Zoe and she made as many moons as you wanted up to a limit of nine, because with more than nine moons it might be as bright at night as it is in the daytime and that would be weird. Zoe's moons came in many colors and sizes. Her online intergalactic planetary business was booming because people hated being outside at night without a moon to light the way.

Harper tapped my shoulder. "Zoe?"

"What?"

"You're doing that daydreaming thing, right?"

"Right," I replied.

"About?" he asked.

"About how many moons we would need to have for there to always be one shining in the sky no matter where you are on Earth."

"Hmmm? That's a really good question. I never thought about that."

"Me neither until just now."

"I always thought you were only interested in plants . . . not moons and planets."

A thought like a small bolt of lightning flashed in my mind. "If you take the *e* out of *planet*, it spells *plant*," I blurted.

"Wow, Zoe, that's pretty good. But then, you're smart like that."

"I am?"

"Yeah. You are."

"Oh. Thanks."

Quiet came after that, the way it does sometimes after serious things are said.

And it was a while before Harper spoke again. "It'd be easier to see up there if we had a telescope."

"I know. I decided to start saving up for one."

Harper glanced at the book, then at me, and said, "Sorry, Zoe."

"For what?"

"For stealing your science idea."

From the way he said it, I could tell he really meant it.

"You promise you'll never do it again?" I asked.

Harper nodded.

"Then I forgive you."

After that, we went inside and Harper said good night to me and I said good night to him.

Later, when my head hit the pillow, I thought about Harper and how it was feeling nice to be okay with him again.

Making peace was VG—very good.

31

Christmas and the Day After

For the first time ever, I could hardly wait for Christmas Day to be over. Quincy was coming tomorrow and staying at our house for the whole week.

Besides, Christmas was becoming like a book I'd practically memorized but I reread over and over again because I liked it so much, year after year after year. Get up in the morning, wish everyone merry Christmas, put on nice clothes, go to church, come home, open presents, say you like it even if you don't, help cook dinner, eat dinner from the fancy plates, help clean up the huge Christmas mess.

We had just finished putting the house back to pre-Christmas normal when suddenly the front door flew open. Daddy bounced up from the sofa, went to the door, and peered outside. "Just the wind," he said. "Santa Anas are kicking up again."

"Toasty outside too," Grandpa Reindeer added.

Grandpa was right. For December, it was pretty hot.

∾

Outside, the wind howled.

The next day, Jade left to spend a few days with her friend Torrey, whose family had a cabin in the mountains, so she wasn't with us when we went to pick up Quincy from the airport.

"Howdeedoo, Mr. Quincy," Daddy said.

He grinned. "Hey, you guys."

"I was thinking we should take advantage of this warm weather and head to the beach. Your mom packed some towels and things. That sound good?" Daddy asked as he pulled out into traffic.

Harper hollered, "Yay!"

"Sounds awesome," Quincy replied.

But I asked, "What about the Wonderland? Who's going to work in the nursery?"

"I closed it for the day. Day after Christmas is always slow, anyway," Daddy answered.

"Can we eat lunch at the beach too?" Harper asked.

Daddy nodded, and before long, we were driving

slowly down the narrow street that leads to Paradise Cove.

"We came here last summer with Wes. They have the best onion rings," I told him.

"But it's kinda expensive," Quincy warned.

Daddy chuckled. "Not to worry. We're here to have a good time."

But as soon as we'd parked, Daddy discovered he'd forgotten his cell phone and started fussing. "What if Jade calls?"

Mom waved her cell phone in his face. "I have mine, Darrow."

Daddy relaxed, squeezing her hand, and we headed into the restaurant, where they took our name and gave us a red lobster thing that would buzz when our table was ready.

"Reindeer? Is that a joke?" the man taking names asked my daddy.

"Not a joke," Daddy informed him.

The man apologized. "Sorry, sir."

"Not a problem," Daddy told him.

Because the man had said the wait for a table for five would be long, we went out the back way and walked to the water's edge. I slipped off my shoes, tied them together, and slung them over my shoulder.

I love the beach, wading in the blue water, watching the sun set, seagulls squawking, the way everyone seems happy.

"I want to live at the beach. Can we please live at the beach?" I pleaded.

"In your dreams," Mom answered.

"When I grow up, I'm going to live at the beach. For real!" I told her, then ran to join Quincy where he and Harper had already planted themselves on the sand.

"Why're you sitting down?" I asked Quincy. "We're at the beach. Let's go!" I reached for his hand, pulled him to his feet, and we waded in the water until it was almost to our knees. The tide rolled out, trying to suck us with it. I wiggled my toes in the wet sand and shielded my eyes from the sun glinting on the water. Some kids with boogie boards paddled out, trying to catch a wave.

Quincy and I stepped out of the cold water and walked onto the warm sand. Every so often, the waves rolled in, licking at our feet. A Frisbee flew by, just missing me.

"How's your friend?" Quincy asked.

"Adam?"

"Yeah, him."

I'd told Quincy about the boy who called me *not ugly* and that mostly we ate lunch together. "He's gone to Paris for vacation, but he's coming back before school starts again," I said. Right then, I wondered if Quincy was making friends too. He hadn't mentioned anything. "Did you get any new friends yet?" I asked.

"Sorta. There's this kid named Simon who lives in the apartment next door and goes to my school. Sometimes when he doesn't have band practice, we walk home together. He plays the trumpet and he's pretty good, except at night when I'm trying to go to sleep and he's practicing, I wish he played a quieter instrument."

"Like a guitar?" I said. "But not electric."

Quincy smiled. "Definitely not electric. That'd be gruesome. And some other kids at school are kinda cool with me, but I haven't, like, gone to their houses or anything."

Although I wanted Quincy to make friends, I wanted to stay his best friend forever. "But I'm still your best friend—right?"

"You know it . . . and I'm still yours?"

I nudged him with my shoulder. "Forever and ever."

Quincy grinned.

All of a sudden, I thought about Kendra. "How's your mom . . . all better?"

"Mostly. She still gets tired sometimes. I've been helping her get organized, as she calls it. And on weekends we kind of explore around, mostly on the BART train."

"Did you ride a trolley car yet?"

Quincy nodded. "And once my mom is a little stronger, we're gonna do the Golden Gate Bridge walk. My dad already jogged across it to Sausalito and back a couple of times."

Zoe, wearing shorts and running shoes, stood on the Golden Gate Bridge, peering out at the horizon. A group of joggers motioned for Zoe to join them. It was a beautiful day in San Francisco. Zoe joined the herd of runners and soon led the pack.

Right then, someone tugged so hard on my T-shirt that I almost fell backward. It was Harper. "C'mon. Our table's ready."

We ordered a bunch of food, ate it all, including dessert, then headed back to the beach. Together, we trailed along, past the big rocks to the tide pools.

The red-orange sun was almost down when the Reindeer parents decided it was time to go.

"Can we please just watch the sun until it disappears?" I begged. "I like the way it looks."

Quincy snapped a photo. "Me too."

"Okay, but after that we need to go," Mom told us. "Battery on my cell just died and I forgot my car charger."

So, as soon as the sun left, we did too.

On the ride home, Harper stared silently out the window, his forehead pressed to the glass. Soft music from the radio played and Mom hummed along. I glanced over at Quincy. He had nodded off. The freeway was backed up and traffic was very slow. I was almost glad it was taking a long time. This had been one of my best days ever and I really didn't want it to be over.

32

Wind and Tears

The closer we got to Pasadena, the stronger the Santa Ana winds got.

We were getting near the Wonderland when the air turned smoky. Ashes floated down on the car's hood and front window, reminding me of snowflakes.

"Musta been a fire," Daddy said. "Wind and heat. Recipe for a blaze."

And then we turned the corner and Daddy skidded to a stop. Fire trucks were everywhere, lining our street. One long red fire truck blocked the road, preventing us from going any farther. A guy in a red SUV that said FIRE CAPTAIN on the door waved us to the side of the road.

Daddy pulled over and rolled down the window. "What happened?"

"A few houses burned down to the ground. That Wonderland plant place too. It's mostly gone. From what we can put together, it started from some candles the old lady was burning. They found her outside her house with the hose, trying to put the fire out. With these winds, it's lucky we stopped it before it did any more damage. Shame right after Christmas. You live around here?"

Daddy put his head down on the steering wheel.

Mom gasped and started to cry.

Harper yelled, "No way!"

I turned to Quincy. "Huh?" was the only sound I could make.

❧

After that, so many things happened that it was hard to keep track.

Because the people from the fire department wouldn't even let us get anywhere close to the Wonderland that night, we headed to Grandpa and Nana's apartment.

Grandpa opened the door. His face had a bad look, a look like he'd just swallowed vinegar.

"It's all gone . . . my whole life." Daddy fell into his father's arms and cried. I don't think I'd ever seen my daddy cry before. I grabbed his hand.

"Went over there as soon as we heard it on the news, but they wouldn't let us near. Sorry you had to find out like that, Darrow. Couldn't get you on your cell phones," Grandpa told him.

Daddy sobbed quietly and Nana and Grandpa Reindeer embraced their only son.

⤫

"It's my fault," I confessed to Quincy later that night as we stared up at the dark ceiling from sleeping bags on Nana and Grandpa's floor.

He nudged me with his arm. "You weren't even there."

"But she started a fire before and I should have told someone, but Mrs. Warner begged me not to because she was afraid they'd put her in an old-people orphanage, and now her house is gone and ours is too. I should have told," I sniveled.

"It's not your fault, Zoe. Really, it's just . . . an accident."

"But . . ."

He tried hard to convince me. "Even if you had

told, it probably still would have happened. I swear it's not your fault," he repeated.

I wanted to believe him but couldn't.

I tossed around all night, barely sleeping. My eyes were wide open when the sun came up. I smelled bacon cooking. I didn't want to be hungry, but I was.

33

The Wonderland's Ashes

*Y*ou would have thought that because the Wonderland had so many amazing things that its ashes would have been special, but they weren't. They were the same as fireplace ashes or the ashes in the barbecue pit: just plain old gray ashes.

Together, the Reindeer family—except for Jade, who was still in the mountains—staggered around through the Wonderland, hoping something hadn't been eaten by the flames. But it seemed like everything had.

Daddy and Mom's faces were as gray as the ashes.

Every tree and plant had been burned to a crisp. The nursery was burned to the ground, and the place where our house had been was charred black.

Quincy and I headed to what was left of the greenhouse. Only one part was still there, but from what I could see, none of the plants had survived.

Then I glanced over to where I'd planted the baobabs. The old coffee cans didn't look like they'd been touched by the fire. I went over and examined the cans one by one.

"Quincy!" I screamed.

He ran to my side. "Are you dying? Because that was an I-am-dying scream."

I held up one of the cans for him to see. It was the old, rusty Kona Hawaiian Coffee can. "One of them finally grew! A baobab!"

We looked at the bright green stem and two perfectly sprouted leaves.

"Wow!" he declared, and snapped a picture.

I didn't think about anything after that. My feet took over and I ran. I had to show Daddy. I found him standing where the nursery used to be. "Daddy!" I yelled.

"What's wrong, Zoe?"

I held up the can for him to see. "It grew. A baobab. It was a secret and I was hoping it would grow by Christmas so I could give it to you for a present, but it didn't. It's a baobab and it's endangered. And it's special. And it's the only thing that didn't get burned up. Merry Christmas!"

Daddy took it from my hand and studied the can and the seedling. "It's a sign," he said. "It has to be a sign."

34

Reindeer in Hawaii

$\mathcal{I}$mmediately after the fire, like vultures circling a dead thing, the land developers arrived, each one offering more and more money for Doc Reindeer's Exotic Plant Wonderland. I don't know how much it got sold for, but I'd overheard Mom say it was enough for us to buy another house with money to spare.

In no time flat, the Wonderland had been bulldozed and cleared.

It was a very sad day seeing it that way, like it suddenly wasn't wearing any clothes.

Other things changed fast too. Mrs. Warner, because she had no family and nowhere else to live, had finally wound up in an old-people orphanage. We'd visited her there one day. It was pretty nice and she seemed sort of happy. At least she wasn't alone anymore. She didn't say anything about the fire. I supposed she didn't remember. Mom said it was just as well. Mrs. Warner had enough bad memories in her life.

Ultimately, I'd confessed to Daddy about that first fire at her house, expecting him to be mad, but Daddy had just shrugged and said, "It's not your fault, Zoe. What's past is past."

Everyone had different ideas about where we should move to, but Daddy claimed the *sign*—the only living thing left after the fire, the baobab growing inside the Hawaiian Coffee can—had made it as clear as glass. It had pointed him toward the path we were supposed to take: the path that led to a flower farm on the island of Kauai in Hawaii.

Now I understood what he meant by a sign.

And no matter how many times Jade yelled, "My life is ruined! I hate you," there was nothing she could do to change his mind.

The entire Reindeer family, including Nana and Grandpa, was moving thousands of miles across the Pacific Ocean.

The flower farm was even more acres than the

Wonderland, plus this house had an attached apartment called an 'ohana unit for Nana and Grandpa. Nearby, there was a botanical garden.

Every time Quincy called on his mom's or dad's cell, all he seemed to talk about was coming to Hawaii to visit during the summer. Kendra had thousands of frequent flier miles. But the summer seemed a long way away. Maybe I'd make at least one new friend before then, I hoped.

༄

In February, on my last day of school in Pasadena, I stood outside with Adam. "Bye," I told him. It was pretty hard saying that word to him, but nowhere near as hard as when Quincy had left.

He took my hand and squeezed it tight. "Bye, Zoe. It'll be an adventure."

"My first," I told him.

"Yes, and maybe I'll get to come to Hawaii someday and visit you. It's on my list of places to go," Adam said.

"You have a list?"

He nodded. "Not exactly a list, but a map of the world. I have a bunch of yellow pushpins stuck in all the places I want to go to, and once I go there, I stick in a red pushpin. You should get a map and put it on your wall."

"That's a good idea . . . I will. Plus maybe we'll come back to California to visit. I'll send you an e-mail when we get there."

"Bye," we said at the same time.

And later that day, when Daddy answered the door at the apartment where the insurance company had paid for us to live after the fire, Ben Rakotomalala was standing there.

"How did you find us?" I asked.

"The man who bought the Wonderland told me," he replied. "I came to express my sorrow and to replace these." He handed me copies of the two books he'd given me. "I assumed they were lost in the fire."

I took them from his hand. "They were . . . Thank you."

Daddy got tears in his eyes. "You're a kind man, Ben."

"We're moving to Kauai in Hawaii. Our plane leaves tomorrow. We bought a flower farm," I blurted.

"The Garden Isle, they call that one. I was there years ago when I worked on the Big Island at the University of Hawaii Institute for Astronomy. If you ever get to the Big Island, you'll have to make sure you visit the Mauna Kea Observatories. By 2022, the island will be home to the world's biggest telescope, allowing scientists to see thirteen billion light-years away."

"Wow!" Harper exclaimed from behind me. Until then, I hadn't known he was even in the room. "Wow!" he repeated. "I cannot wait to see that."

"Well, it's time for me to say my good-byes," the tall man said. His words had a little sadness sprinkled on them.

Daddy glanced at the books I was holding, said, "Thanks again," and shook his hand.

"Bye, and thank you for the books," I told him.

He said good-bye one last time and turned to leave, heading toward the elevator.

Suddenly, I glanced at the baobab seedling in the Kona coffee can that was sitting on the table.

"Daddy? I know it was supposed to be your present, but we can always grow some more, and this time I'll follow the instructions." I picked up the baobab. "Can I give this one to Ben? Please? I promised him."

"Ben!" Daddy called out. "Hold up! My Zoe has a gift for you."

I flew down the hallway to Ben Rakotomalala. "It's a baobab. For you."

He took the can from my hand. "Thank you, Zoe!"

"Don't water it too much or it might die," I warned him.

The elevator came and he waved at my daddy. "Thank you again, Zoe."

"You're welcome . . . I won't forget you," I said as he stepped inside the elevator.

"Nor I you, Zoe Reindeer," he replied.

The elevator door was closing when he stopped it with his hand and it reopened. Ben stared into my eyes. "One more thing, Zoe. Promise you'll put that wonderful imagination of yours to good use."

"I promise."

The elevator door closed and the tall man from Madagascar disappeared from sight.

Back inside the apartment, I plopped on the sofa beside Harper and together we flipped open the book by Carl Sagan, *Cosmos.*

Just like before, Ben had written on the first page:

To My Friend Zoe Reindeer—May your life be an amazing adventure.

Ben Rakotomalala

35

Zoe G. Reindeer's First Adventure

The next morning, Jade had to practically be dragged to the airport. "It's all your fault, plant girl! You and your seeds!" she hollered at me for what seemed like the hundredth time.

"That's enough, Jade!" Daddy told her. "It's not Zoe's fault."

It kind of is, I thought. I remembered the things that were definitely my fault and the things that weren't and how, when you combine some of those things, they're what brought the Reindeer family to Hawaii. Like if I had never bought the seeds, we probably wouldn't be moving to Hawaii. But everyone except Jade seemed really happy about it, including Harper.

"It's an adventure," I said, hoping Jade might start to see it the way I did.

But Jade was too full of anger, and she growled at me like she was part animal.

I supposed anger keeps you from seeing through another person's eyes, like when I was so mad at Harper. But finally there'd been an end to the Harper-Zoe battle, and I wondered if sometime soon there'd be an end to the Jade-Zoe war and we'd have some peace too. I hoped so.

On the ride and while we waited inside the airport terminal, she completely stopped talking. But I couldn't feel too sorry for her, because I knew that as soon as we landed, she'd start collecting friends again like they were refrigerator magnets.

We boarded, and the minute I sat down, I buckled my seat belt. I'd really been looking forward to doing that. I, Zoe G. Reindeer, was on my first plane ride. The captain welcomed us over the speaker. It was just the way I'd always imagined it would be. Only this was real and real was a million times better.

The plane took off and I stared back at California, wondering if I'd migrate back there someday—maybe, maybe not.

The ocean was blue beneath us, but soon we were above the clouds and I couldn't see it anymore. Yet the star of day was up there, shining bright as could be. I had promised myself to stay awake for the entire ride. I really didn't want to miss a thing, but I'd hardly slept last night because I was extremely excited, so after I ate a sandwich, sleep finally got me.

∼

"Wake up, Zoe." Nana, who was sitting beside me, poked me gently awake.

"Huh?" I said sleepily.

"We're almost there, getting ready to land. You don't want to miss this. Hawaii is about to get something slightly unusual."

"What?" I asked.

Nana grinned. "Reindeer . . . a whole family of them."

"You're silly, Nana," I said, nudging her playfully with my shoulder.

I stared out the window at a very green island, a greener place than I'd ever seen. I smiled at Nana. Before I knew it, the plane had landed and come to a stop. I wanted to be the first one off, nevertheless I had to wait like almost everyone else. But waiting didn't bother me. It was my first adventure and I wanted to remember every minute of it.

36

A New Wonderland

On the drive to our new Wonderland, there were beaches with clear blue water and green forests lining both sides of the highway. It was as beautiful as anything *Imaginary Zoe* ever experienced.

Finally we reached our farm. I recognized the black wrought-iron gate with the lotus flower design from the pictures I'd seen. I glanced back at Jade and was happy to see that even she was smiling.

As soon as we were out of the car, everyone except for me headed inside to check out the house. But there was something else I needed to do first. Weeks ago, I'd sent away for more baobab seeds. I patted the seed packet I'd put in my jeans pocket and took off to explore.

According to Daddy, Hawaii, being a tropical island, might be a good place for the baobabs to grow. And from what I'd read online, I'd learned he was right, because Hawaii already had a few. I knew I needed to start them in small pots before I transferred them outside, and now that I'd actually read the directions, this time it wasn't going to take forever for them to sprout. But what I was looking for was the perfect spot to grow them, and before long, I found it. The grass was high and green and the red earth was moist. It reminded me of the land in the picture of the baobabs in Madagascar. Only one thing was different: the sky was so much bluer. This was the place, I decided, where I would grow them. The baobabs would certainly like it here. I patted the seeds again. Today, I'd soak them in water, and tomorrow, I'd find some pots and plant them. I couldn't wait to tell Quincy. He and Kendra were planning to visit this coming summer, and I hoped the baobabs would be big enough by that time for him to help me transplant them to their special place.

Walking back toward the house, I thought about being like a seed and how some, like the baobab seeds, took longer than usual to germinate and sprout. It felt like I'd finally sprouted too.

Now not just my feet and bones were growing—in

other ways that seemed to be invisible, I was changing day by day. I wasn't so shy anymore, and because of Adam and Mrs. Warner, I knew I wasn't ugly and that I was even nice. I was actually looking forward to making friends. And I was happy that Harper and I were getting close again and, because of Ben Rakotomalala, I was getting more interested in all kinds of science stuff—not just plants but outer space too.

And like a baobab, I am slightly unusual. I'm a Reindeer in Hawaii. My name finally made sense—a slightly unusual name for a slightly unusual girl. "Zoe G. Reindeer," I said out loud, then put my lips together to try and whistle. For the first time, a sound came out. I couldn't believe it. I pursed my lips and blew again. As sweetly as birdsong, a whistle flew out of me. I was more than surprised. I was astonished.

Later that night, I stood outside alone on the outdoor patio that wraps around the house, called the lanai. I gazed out toward the ocean where the light from the Moon glistened and thought about the promise I'd made to Ben to make good use of my imagination. I didn't know exactly how, but deep inside I knew that I would keep that promise.

But for right now, real seemed like it was more

than a million times better than anything my imagination could come up with.

Right now, real was amazing.

Inside, I heard the whole Reindeer family laughing loudly about something, even Jade.

Zoe G. Reindeer headed in to join them, whistling a tune.

Acknowledgments

$\mathcal{S}$ome of the inspiration for this book came from George Washington Carver, a premier American botanist, and a JPL plasma physicist, Dr. Claudia Alexander—both gone on to a peaceful pasture but never to be forgotten.

A thousand and one thanks to Nancy Paulsen for her expertly deft editorial hand. Additional thanks to Sara LaFleur, Frank Morrison for his wonderful jacket, the copy editor, and all of the people at Penguin Random House who worked behind the scenes to bring Zoe G. Reindeer from where she began as a spark in my mind into the hands of readers.

As always, I give thanks to the Spirit. As a species, our capacity for compassion remains great.

Also by Brenda Woods

The Blossoming Universe of Violet Diamond

CCBC Choice

***Kirkus* Best Book**

★ "Violet's a bright, engaging biracial preteen. . . . Infused
with humor, hope and cleareyed compassion—a fresh take on
an old paradigm."—*Kirkus Reviews*, starred review

★ "Endearing. . . . Admirably touches upon profound issues related
to identity and race and tenderly conveys intergenerational bonds."
—*School Library Journal*, starred review

"Deftly raises complex issues of race and identity and leaves them open
for discussion: whether race matters, what makes a family, how it feels
to be different, and what it means to be biracial."—*Publishers Weekly*

"Violet is a winning protagonist, full of questions and full of hope.
She's believably complex . . . a sometimes shy, sometimes sparkly
and strong person to whom many readers will relate."
—*The Bulletin of the Center for Children's Books*

Saint Louis Armstrong Beach

Chicago Public Library's Best of the Best Reading List

ALAN (Assembly on Literature for Adolescents) Pick

★ "Gripping. . . . Woods's marvelous characterizations of Saint and
Miz Moran more than stand up to the vivid backdrop of the flooded,
chaotic city. . . . A small gem that sparkles with hope, resilience and
the Crescent City's unique, jazz-infused spirit."
—*Kirkus Reviews*, starred review

★ "With his engaging voice, readers will quickly take a shine
to Saint. . . . Woods skillfully provides a sense of the growing
tension. . . . While the tragedy of the event is not glossed over,
the overall theme is one of hope."
—*School Library Journal*, starred review

★ "The characters are well-developed, and readers truly will care
about their fates."—*Library Media Connection*, starred review

"Moving. . . . Vividly portrays the force of the storm, and the
authentic New Orleans setting works as a powerful character,
adding an extra dimension to this compelling Katrina story."
—*The Horn Book*

෴

My Name Is Sally Little Song

Book Sense Pick

Book Links Best Books for the Classroom

★ "True to the child's voice, the terse, first-person narrative . . .
brings close the backbreaking labor and cruelty of plantation life,
then the flight to freedom, the sadness, and the hope. The action is
fast, the journey fraught with danger; the details bring it home. . . . The
searing historical fiction shows that there can be no sunny ending."
—*Booklist*, starred review

"A believable, horrifying portrayal of life as a captive. . . .
Involving and bittersweet."—*Publishers Weekly*

"Provides readers with an alternative view of the realities of
slavery. . . . Deftly teases out both the light and the dark
moments of the experience. . . . This accessible tale will prove
a rich resource for study and discussion."—*School Library Journal*

❧

The Red Rose Box

Coretta Scott King Honor

PEN Center USA Literary Award Finalist

FOCAL Award

Judy Lopez Memorial Award

IRA Notable Books for a Global Society List

"Beautifully and accurately evokes a particularly painful and hopeful time through an insider's eyes, and yet it is also a timeless, universal tale of a young girl's road to maturity. An impressive debut."
—*Kirkus Reviews*

"Well-realized, believable characters. Ruth is the embodiment of a sassy eight-year-old and the adults are genuine, loving, and supportive. . . . Ends on a hopeful note and will appeal to readers."
—*School Library Journal*

"Moving. . . . [Woods] creates some memorable characters . . . and probes historical events in a personal context that may open many readers' eyes."—*Publishers Weekly*

"Language made musical with southern phrases . . . shapes the era and characters with both well-chosen particulars and universal emotions. . . . Young readers will connect with Leah and feel her difficult pull between freedom, comfort, and her deeply felt roots."—*Booklist*

Turn the page to read the first chapters of

THE BLOSSOMING UNIVERSE OF
Violet Diamond

1

THE PUZZLING UNIVERSE
OF VIOLET DIAMOND

Did you ever have a dream that's so good, you wish you could save it forever instead of having it go back to that place in your mind where dreams become quieter than whispers, quiet like snowflakes falling?

And it's such an awesome dream that makes you so happy that right after you wake up, you rush to write it down because you can't just let it evaporate into nothing?

Did you ever have a dream like that? Last night, I did.

In my dream I was walking along one of those picture-perfect beaches you see in vacation ads, where seals sunbathe on rocks and tropical fish swim in see-through-blue water. In the distance, dolphins leaped from the ocean, and even though it was daytime and the sun was shining bright, a crescent moon hung in the sky. My mom was on one side, my dad on the other, holding my hands. Daisy, my older sister, was walking ahead of us. In my dream we all looked alike, same skin, same hair, same big white teeth that gleam when we smile.

Barefoot people walked by us on the beach and smiled. Everyone could tell, just by looking at us, we were a family. There were no question marks in their eyes, no looks on their faces that remind me of puzzles with missing pieces, no under-the-microscope stares.

But the absolute best part of the dream was that my dad was there with us. I snuggled close to him, his arm hugged my shoulder, and he looked at me with love in his eyes.

And then, my alarm went off and I woke up. Outside, the rain was pouring and a nearby lightning strike lit my room like a camera flash.

I grabbed my 500-page journal where I write down words I've never heard before along with their definitions, lists of all sorts of things, and my wishes that never seem to come true. I read the first wish I'd ever written.

1. I Wish My Dad Was Alive Instead of Dead.

Somehow, my wish had found its way into my dream.

I flipped to some blank pages at the back, started a new section called *Dreams I Always Want to Remember,* and began scribbling down the dream. Suddenly, I stopped writing and thought about the dream at the beach, my dad holding my hand, the smile that was in his eyes. Father's Day, a day I sometimes wish didn't exist, was coming up. I could feel my dream happiness vanish and the sadness coming, and even though I tried hard not to let them, all at once the gloomy clouds from outside got sucked in through my ears and invaded my brain. Did you know violets actually shrink? They do, and I did.

2

A PREDICTABLE SUMMER
OF BORING NOTHING

Tomorrow was the last day of school before summer vacation, but my best friend, Athena, was leaving tonight for Greece, where her grandparents live in a house that overlooks the beach. Lucky for her but unlucky for me because it meant I'd have a whole summer without my best friend. It was no secret that I wished I was going with her.

A dead and dull summertime awaits me.

Lately, I'd been imagining all of the boring nothing I was going to fill the summer with. *If boredom was something you eat,* I wondered, *what would it taste like?* Maybe like chicken broth when you're sick, mashed potatoes without gravy, or macaroni minus the cheese.

The sky was blue and it was a little hot except under the

shade of trees. "My mom said I could have a cat this morning," I told Athena as we strolled along home from school.

Athena smiled. "She finally said yes?"

"Yep. She must have gotten tired of me begging all the time. She's going to take me to the shelter."

"A recycled pet?" Athena smiled again. There is one thing Athena Starros is full of—smiles.

I nodded. "We might go this weekend."

Athena flipped her long, straight, light brown hair. "My cousin had a cat and once it pooped in her bed. She forgot to make her bed one day, and that night, when she climbed into bed, she got cat poop all over her. Gross. Plus they caught the cat eating the Thanksgiving turkey that they'd left on the table after dinner and had to throw it away. Also gross. And then they found it in the crib with her baby brother and her dad decided it had to go."

"I'm still getting a cat, Athena."

"Just saying. Pets are a lot of work." Another thing Athena is full of—advice.

"Some pets," I corrected her.

"They should have a place where you could rent a pet for maybe a week, and if you like it you can keep it, but if you don't you can bring it back." Sometimes Athena talks too much and this was definitely one of those times. "Plus cats are boring, don't you think?" she added.

"Yep, usually they're quiet." I stopped walking and put my finger to my mouth as if to say shhh.

Athena got the hint and changed the subject. "We might go to Italy for a week. My grandma wants me to see Rome."

"Yay! Athena goes to Rome. I'll be thinking about that while I'm in my room with my boring cat and stinky litter box all summer."

Athena made a sad face. "Sorry . . . Wish you could come, too, V."

Because I knew she meant it, I smiled. But in my mind, I daydreamed that I was going with her. Then, I silently wished I had grandparents who lived far away and wanted me to come for a long visit. All I have are Gam and Poppy, who live right around the corner.

My thoughts must have shown on my face, because Athena blurted, "Would you stop the sad looks? I'll keep in touch. Plus, it's not like you're friendless . . . you still have Yaz," she reminded me.

Yaz, short for Yazmine, is my kinda-sorta-good friend, a girl who doesn't go to school with us but who I know from the ice skating rink. For Yaz Kilroy, ice skating is everything.

"But she hardly ever does regular stuff like us, only skating," I said.

Athena agreed, "Yeah, I know."

A little silence followed.

"You're flying all the way by yourself, huh?"

Athena put out her hand and shook it nervously. "For the first time."

In minutes, we reached her house, which is right down the street from mine.

"You gotta send me a gazillion postcards like you said. And if you meet a cute boy, promise not to forget about me like Daisy." Since my sister, Daisy, got her new boy-friend, Wyatt, it seemed like she barely had time for me anymore. Another reason I could safely predict this was going to be a summer of boring nothing.

"I won't," Athena promised, and we stared at each other for what seemed like a long time until tears got in our eyes.

Finally, Athena gave me a big bright grin and hugged me tight.

I smiled what Poppy calls a counterfeit smile, day-dreamed once more that I was going with her, said good-bye, and headed home.

If boredom was like macaroni without cheese, what I felt right then was worse. Lemonade without sugar, soda without the fizz. Pitiful.

3

SOMETIMES I WISH

With Athena gone, I was walking home alone from my last day of elementary school when just like that, dark gray clouds that mean it's going to rain for certain gathered and turned the almost-summer air cold. I didn't have my umbrella and wasn't even wearing a hoodie. Lucky Violet.

I needed to run fast and that's exactly what I was about to do when I heard what sounded like crying, so I stopped and listened. There it was again—not a cry, a cat's meow. I followed the mews until I found it curled up under a tree in front of a house, a kitten with spotted fur, almost like a leopard. I kneeled down and gently stroked its little head, but the kitten's eyes were crusted shut and wouldn't open. I dug through my backpack, found a napkin, dampened it with water from my water bottle, and carefully wiped away the crust. Before long, it opened its eyes, and I smiled because the kitten's eyes were hazel . . . the same green-blue-brown color eyes as my mom's and Daisy's.

"How did you get here?" I asked as I picked it up and cradled it like a baby. I had been wishing for a cat for months. Maybe we wouldn't have to get one from the shelter after all. Was it possible that one of my wishes was finally coming true? I smiled inside and out.

The kitten opened its mouth wide and let out a really loud "Meow!"

"You sure are a loud mouth."

Again, "Meow!" This time louder and longer.

"A really loud mouth," I proclaimed.

The sound of a door opening made me turn toward the house I was standing in front of. An old lady peeked out. "What you got there, Curly?" she asked.

My hair is long and—guess what—curly. No, not just curly—corkscrew curly. And if one more person calls me Curly, I'm going to scream.

"A kitten," I replied.

"That so?" the woman said as she came outside and hobbled with a cane down her walkway toward me. Her short hair was snow white and her skin so wrinkly, it looked like someone had ironed creases in it.

Please don't let the kitten belong to her.

She stared at the kitten for a while, then stroked its spotted fur. "Where do you suppose it came from?"

I sighed. "It's not yours?"

"No, not mine." She grinned at the kitten, then at me. "Looks hungry, though. Maybe needs some milk." She began walking back to her door. "C'mon, Curly."

"My name's Violet, not Curly," I informed her as I grabbed my backpack and trailed her to the door.

"Well, c'mon, Vi," she said.

"It's not Vi, either, just Violet, or call me V. That's what most people call me."

"I like Violet better," the old lady commented as she reached to open the screen door.

"That's how it is these days, kind of. I mean, lots of people call other people by the first initial of their name. Like, instead of calling my sister Daisy, I call her D."

"Violet and Daisy? Your parents must have a penchant for flowers."

Penchant? I'd have to add that to my book of words I'd never heard before. "What's a penchant?"

"Means 'a strong liking for something.'" She paused. "But violet's also a color . . . reddish blue."

"It's also the name for a small butterfly that belongs to the family Lycaenidae." I love telling people that because it usually makes them think I'm incredibly smart. I could tell by the look in her eyes that this lady was instantly added to my list of *people who think Violet Diamond is incredibly smart.*

"Really? I didn't know that. So you're an entomologist."

"A person who studies insects? Nope . . . I seriously hate bugs. Seriously."

Her face crinkled into a smile. "Me too," she agreed as she motioned me inside. "Wipe your feet."

The old lady seemed pretty normal, but no way was I going inside a stranger's house. "I'll wait here," I told her.

"Okay, Violet . . . or V."

"What's your name?" I asked.

"Georgina," she replied.

"So, I might just call you G. Get it?"

She grinned and her eyes, which were as blue as Gam's, sparkled. "Got it," she replied, stepping inside the house.

Before long, she came back with a small bowl of milk, but her hands were pretty shaky and some of it spilled as she set it down. "Getting old."

I put the kitten down and nudged it close to the bowl. Quickly, it lapped the milk, and when it seemed like it was full, the spotted kitty sat back and let out another extremely loud meow.

"Loud mouth," I said.

"So you could name it LM for Loud Mouth," G suggested.

I hadn't even thought about a name. "LM? It's not

really a cat name," I said, then asked, "So you think I should keep it? I mean, do you think it belongs to someone around here?"

"So many strays around here, it's a crime. Save me from having to call Animal Control one more time. Yes, V, I definitely think you should keep it, if it's okay with your parents."

"It's just my mom."

"Oh," G said with a sad voice, the way some grownups do when I tell them that "it's just my mom."

When G opened her mouth to talk again, I figured *here come the questions. Not today,* I thought. May as well tell her. "My dad is dead." G's eyes looked the way my insides suddenly felt, sad. "But I have a really nice grandpa," I added. The old lady's eyes turned happy. That should be the end of that, I hoped.

It was, because G sighed, "That's nice."

Right then thunder clapped. Before long, it was going to pour.

Georgina gazed up. "You hurry home now, V," she ordered.

I scooped up the kitten and was busy thanking G for the milk when humungous drops of rain began polka-dotting the street, sidewalk, and walkway. It was only three blocks to my house, but still, no matter how fast I ran, I was bound to get soaked.

Just as I prepared to bolt, Georgina asked, "Don't you have an umbrella?"

I shook my head. "No."

"Wait here. I have extras."

Around here, most people have more than one umbrella. My grandpa claims that in our town, Moon Lake, Washington, umbrellas are big business. Moon Lake is not too far from Seattle. In Moon Lake, it rains—a lot.

While G was inside, I carefully placed the kitten in my backpack. "We'll be home soon," I said. Another very loud meow.

"Thank you," I told the lady when she handed me the umbrella. "I'll bring it back tomorrow . . . I promise."

"Keep it. I have a grand collection."

I thanked her again, opened the umbrella, clutched the backpack to my chest with one arm, and took off.